Never Stop Singing

A Melody Classic
Volume 2

by Denise Lewis Patrick

★ American Girl®

Published by American Girl Publishing

16 17 18 19 20 21 LEO 10 9 8 7 6 5 4 3 2 1

All American Girl marks, BeForever™, Melody™,
and Melody Ellison™ are trademarks of American Girl.

Grateful acknowledgment is made to the following for permission to quote
previously published material: "Dream Boogie" and "Youth" from
THE COLLECTED POEMS OF LANGSTON HUGHES by Langston Hughes,
edited by Arnold Rampersad with David Roessel, Associate Editor,
copyright © 1994 by the Estate of Langston Hughes. Used by permission of
Alfred A. Knopf, an imprint of the Knopf Doubleday Publishing Group, a
division of Penguin Random House LLC. All rights reserved. Any third-party
use of this material, outside of this publication, is prohibited. Interested parties
must apply directly to Penguin Random House LLC for permission.

Cover image by Michael Dwornik and Juliana Kolesova
Author photo by Fran Baltzer Photo

Cataloging-in-Publication Data available from the Library of Congress

americangirl.com/service

This book is dedicated in friendship to
Sharon Shavers Gayle
and in gratitude to the unforgettable
Mr. Horace Julian Bond

Beforever™

The adventurous characters you'll meet in
the BeForever books will spark your curiosity
about the past, inspire you to find your voice
in the present, and excite you about your future.
You'll make friends with these girls as you share
their fun and their challenges. Like you, they are
bright and brave, imaginative and energetic,
creative and kind. Just as you are, they are
discovering what really matters: Helping others.
Being a true friend. Protecting the earth.
Standing up for what's right. Read their stories,
explore their worlds, join their adventures.
Your friendship with them will BeForever.

♫ TABLE *of* CONTENTS ♫

When Melody's story takes place, the terms "Negro," "colored," and "black" were all used to describe Americans of African descent. You'll see all of those words used in this book.

Today, "Negro" and "colored" can be offensive because they are associated with racial inequality. "African American" is a more contemporary term, but it wasn't commonly used until the late 1980s.

Melody's Eve

melody Ellison stared for a moment at the bright new calendar in her hands before she put it up on the kitchen wall. The picture on the January page showed a tall evergreen tree, its thick branches frosted with snow.

"*O Christmas tree, O Christmas tree, how lovely are your branches,*" Melody sang, even though Christmas had been over for a week. It was New Year's Eve, and tomorrow would be the first day of 1964, her tenth birthday!

Melody loved the idea that having a New Year's birthday meant that the whole world was having a birthday, too. Until now she'd been too young to stay awake past midnight, or to attend the special Watch Night service at their church. Now that she was turning ten, her parents had decided that she was old enough to do both.

"Dee-Dee's almost double digits!" Her sister Lila playfully tugged at one of Melody's braids, then reached into the refrigerator and got out the eggs.

"That's right!" Melody said proudly. Lila was already thirteen, and Melody somehow felt as if she was finally catching up.

"Good morning, Melody," her mother said, joining the girls in the kitchen. "I see you're carrying on your calendar-changing tradition!" Bo, the family's black-and-white mixed terrier, ran in at her heels.

"Yes, I am, Mommy," Melody said, watching her mother tie on a colorful apron. "Are you about to make my birthday cake?" Her mother's triple-chocolate layer cakes were so good that Melody couldn't imagine celebrating anything special without one.

"We are." Mommy set ingredients on the table: butter, sugar, baking powder, cocoa. Bo must have guessed that something good was coming, because he began to bark. Melody bent down to pet him, and Bo flopped onto his side, waving one paw in the air.

Mommy took out the large mixing bowl and started sifting flour into it. "Lila, will you separate the eggs?"

"Sure. Five, right?"

Mommy nodded at Lila and smiled. "Why, I think soon you'll be able to make this cake on your own."

"It's more fun to bake with you," Lila said.

One of the things Melody loved most about her family was that they always worked together—to set the table, do chores around the house, or even solve one another's problems. Big Momma, Melody's grandmother, called it "harmony." She was a music teacher, and she said their family was good at putting their voices together to make one great sound. Melody knew that Big Momma didn't just mean singing. She meant they helped and supported one another in all sorts of ways.

"If I weren't going to help Poppa decorate the church hall for tonight, I'd help make the cake," Melody said, standing up.

"Hey! You can't help make your own birthday cake!" Lila said, cracking an egg against the side of a cup. Melody giggled as the egg almost slipped onto the floor. Bo scrambled up and began to bark again.

The soft swishing of the flour sifter stopped, and her mother looked at Melody. "My baby girl is going to be ten tomorrow!" she said. "Seems like it was just yesterday that you were born."

"Mommy, I'm not a baby anymore," Melody reminded her, skipping out to the living room. "I'm about to become double digits, remember?"

Melody glanced at the sunburst clock over the sofa. Her grandfather, Poppa, wouldn't be picking her up for another half hour. She turned the TV on and waited while it warmed up. When the picture appeared, Melody turned the knob through all the channels, looking for something fun to watch. It was morning and there was no school, so she was hoping for cartoons, or at least a music show. Instead, every station seemed to be running a program that looked back on the year's news. Melody didn't really want to be reminded. She reached for the knob to shut the TV off.

"Wait, Dee-Dee!" Melody's other sister Yvonne called out from the stairs. "Don't turn it off. I want to watch."

Yvonne was home from college for the holidays, and Melody was glad to have her back for a few weeks. Now, if only their brother Dwayne were here! This was the first Christmas he'd ever been away, and Melody really missed him. He and his singing group, The

Three Ravens, were traveling around the country singing for Motown, the famous record company. Dwayne was a talented musician, but Daddy didn't like his new career one bit. Dwayne was only eighteen, and Daddy and Mommy wanted him to go to college instead. *It's funny*, Melody thought. *Dwayne's job as a singer isn't bringing much harmony to our family.*

Melody sighed, and together with her sister watched a grainy replay of the new president, Lyndon B. Johnson, being sworn into office in November.

Yvonne shook her head. "I still can't believe somebody shot the president of the United States," she said, turning up the sound. They listened as the grim-faced newscaster told the whole story again: how President John F. Kennedy and the First Lady were in a motorcade in Dallas, Texas, on November 22. They were riding in the back of a Lincoln Continental convertible when a man with a gun fired at the car, killing the president and wounding the governor of Texas.

"The country remains in shock as our new president faces a grieving nation, problems overseas, and growing civil rights protests here at home," said the newscaster. Then he began to talk about the bombing of a Birmingham, Alabama, church in September that had killed four little girls. Melody turned away from the screen. Somebody who wanted to frighten black people away from fighting for equal rights had set off the bomb on a Sunday morning.

Although it had happened miles and miles away from Detroit, Melody had been frightened—so much so that she'd lost her voice right before the big Youth Day concert. For a long while she'd even been afraid to go inside her own church.

"I'll never forget that day," Yvonne said, interrupting Melody's memories.

Melody looked at her sister and remembered that Yvonne had been away at Tuskegee, her college, when it happened. Tuskegee was also in Alabama—only a few hours' drive from Birmingham.

"Vonnie," Melody suddenly asked, "were *you* scared?" She'd never really thought about that before. Yvonne had called to tell their parents that she was all right, but Melody had never considered that her brave big sister might have been frightened, too.

"Well, yes, at first," Yvonne said. "I had signed up to go to Birmingham that very next weekend. We were going to sit in at a lunch counter to protest the fact that they refuse to serve black people. But after that Sunday I was thinking, *What if something awful happens to me and my friends? Maybe I won't go after all.* Then I remembered Mom telling me that I should always stand up to wrong. Bombing that church was wrong. Treating black people unfairly is wrong. So I decided that I had to go to Birmingham and support what I believe in, you know?"

Melody nodded. "Big Momma told me something like that, too! She said we should keep our hearts and voices strong when bad things happen. I tried really hard to be strong for the little girls in Birmingham. I *wanted* to be, only I wasn't sure I could."

Yvonne smiled and gave Melody a hug. "You didn't let fear turn you around, did you?" she said. "You went back to church to sing. You *were* strong."

"I guess . . ." Melody said slowly. Her family and friends had helped her find courage, and her voice, again. But there was another reason she had wanted to sing. "I didn't want to let the choir down," she said.

"That's because you weren't thinking only about yourself," Yvonne said, switching off the TV. "You were thinking about lots of other people, too. Hey, only a responsible person can do that, Dee-Dee."

Melody didn't say anything, but she felt herself smiling. Yvonne had made her feel a little less sad and a little more grown up.

Just then there was a hard knock on the front door. Yvonne answered it, and their grandparents came in, along with a blast of cold air.

"Well, Happy Melody's Eve, everybody!" Poppa's voice boomed. It was his joke to call the day before New Year's "Melody's Eve."

"Hello, my chicks!" Big Momma said, taking off her coat. As Melody hurried to hug them, she noticed the large wrapped box her grandfather had brought in and propped beside the door.

"Poppa, what's that?" Melody asked, peeking curiously at the mysterious package. But when she looked to her grandfather for an answer, he only shrugged.

Big Momma smiled. "Well," she said, "it's a day early, but we brought our birthday girl a little something."

"Ohhh!" Melody gasped at the surprise.

"Wow. That's a pretty big box for a *little* something," Yvonne said.

Melody picked up the box and carried it to the sofa. It wasn't heavy, but it wasn't exactly light, either. She shook it gently, hearing only a soft swish-swishing sound.

"Can I open it right now?" she asked.

"That was the idea, Little One," Poppa laughed. "Go right ahead!"

Melody didn't wait another second. She ripped off the wrapping paper, tugged the top off the box, and peeled back two layers of tissue paper to find a beautiful cream-colored dress with gold lace. It was folded neatly on top of a matching double-breasted coat with gold buttons. Melody looked up, wide-eyed.

"We thought you might like to dress up, since it's your first Watch Night and Melody's Eve all rolled into one," Poppa told her.

"Do you like them?" Big Momma asked.

Melody nodded. "I've never owned anything so fancy," she said. "Thank you!"

"Dee-Dee, try the coat on!" Yvonne said.

Melody eagerly slipped into the coat and felt warm

all over. The cream-colored collar and cuffs were soft against her skin. She held her arms out and did a little twirl across the living room floor.

Big Momma clapped. "A perfect fit!"

"I could be a model in the *Ebony* magazine Fashion Fair," Melody said proudly.

"You can be anything you want to be," Yvonne said seriously.

Melody thought about their earlier conversation and smiled at her sister's compliment.

Poppa cleared his throat. "How about being my helper in getting the church decorated for tonight? Or did that fancy coat make you forget?" he teased.

"Oh, no, Poppa," Melody said quickly. "I'll be ready in just a minute." She carefully took off her new coat and started to fold it back into the box.

"Let me hang those up for you," Yvonne offered. "So they don't wrinkle."

Melody handed her sister the coat and the box and followed Poppa to the front door. She grabbed her old jacket from the hook and then turned back to her grandmother.

"I love my birthday present. Thank you!"

♪ Melody's Eve ♪

"I'm so glad," Big Momma told her. "You'll look beautiful. Now you two go and make our New Hope church beautiful for tonight, too."

"We will!" Melody said enthusiastically.

Poppa's truck was in the driveway. The words "Frank's Flowers" were on the passenger door. Poppa owned a flower shop on 12th Street, and he had taught Melody everything she knew about plants and gardening.

Melody climbed into the truck and peeked through the back window to see evergreen branches just like the ones on the kitchen calendar. "Oh, Poppa! The hall is going to smell so good!" Melody said. One of her favorite things about this time of year—besides her birthday—was the strong scent of evergreens.

"Yep. I have flowers, too," Poppa said. "Poinsettias and amaryllis. We'll make things look real nice for this evening. Are you excited about your first Watch Night service?"

Melody knew from her brother and sisters that Watch Night wouldn't exactly be a New Year's Eve party like the ones that were on TV. But there would be singing, and preaching by Pastor Daniels, with food and fellowship afterward in the church hall.

"I'm glad I can finally wait up with everybody else till midnight," she told him. "But why isn't it called 'Wait Night' instead of 'Watch Night'?"

"Well, Watch Night is a tradition for some colored folks, especially those of us with family in the South. It goes back a hundred years, when word got out ahead of time that President Abraham Lincoln planned to announce to the country that all slaves were free. The president was going to make the announcement on New Year's Day, 1863. So colored people, slave and free, sat up all night, keeping watch for freedom—Watch Night."

"But you can't *see* freedom," Melody said.

"Are you sure about that?" Poppa asked.

Melody wondered for a moment what freedom might look like. Would it look like the thousands of people who had marched in Washington, D.C., last August? Or maybe like Detroit's own Walk to Freedom in June? Melody and her family had joined thousands of others to hear Dr. Martin Luther King Jr. speak.

"Would freedom look like people of all races, doing things together?" she asked.

"Maybe," Poppa said, glancing at her. "Back in 1863, *that* kind of freedom was just a dream. But I think on that first Watch Night, they could see freedom coming. How many times have you tried to stay awake on Melody's Eve, because what's coming is so special? When you're expecting something big, something wonderful to happen, you can't rest. And when that Emancipation Proclamation did come, our people celebrated. We've been giving thanks ever since, during Watch Night."

"Wow," Melody murmured. She was thankful that she was finally going to stay up for Watch Night. And she was proud that her birthday was linked to such an important tradition.

Watch Night

*A*t eleven-thirty that night, Melody walked into New Hope Baptist Church wearing her birthday dress and coat. She felt as if she sparkled as she settled into her seat between Lila and Yvonne. She had sat between her sisters ever since she was a tiny girl. Now, half an hour away from turning ten, Melody felt very grown up.

She inhaled the spicy smell of the pine branches she and Poppa had woven into a garland across the choir stand up front. As she watched for Poppa and Big Momma and her cousins to arrive, Melody glanced around at everything else that was so familiar: the beautiful stained-glass windows, the many faces she'd known forever. New Hope Baptist Church had always been her home away from home. There had been a time, right after the church bombing in Birmingham, that being here had frightened her, but now New Hope made Melody feel safe again.

When her cousin Val and the rest of the family arrived, they all oohed and aahed over Melody's dress and coat. "It was so hard not to tell you about them," Val said after she'd talked Lila into letting her sit next to Melody.

"You knew about it?" Melody asked.

Val grinned. "Surprise!" she giggled. Val and her parents were staying with Poppa and Big Momma until they could find a house of their own. They'd moved to Detroit from Birmingham in May, and it was taking them a long time to buy a house.

Before Melody could ask Val anything else, Pastor Daniels stepped up to the pulpit.

"Good evening!" the preacher said. His voice was always loud and clear, and he never needed to use a microphone.

"Good evening!" everyone answered together.

Pastor Daniels peered out at the crowd over the tops of his glasses. "A week ago, many of us received gifts," he began. "Isn't that right?"

"Yes, sir!" a young voice answered from the back.

A few people laughed, and Melody turned to look.

Pastor Daniels chuckled before he continued. "Well, New Hope church family, at midnight everyone here will receive another gift. When the New Year comes in, each of us will receive a new opportunity to make a difference in the world. That's a special gift. And I want each one of you to ask yourself: What will I do with *my* gift? What will *I* do to help justice, equality, and dignity grow in our community?"

Melody sat up a little straighter. She thought of the seeds she and Poppa planted in their gardens every spring and of the work it took to make those seeds grow and blossom. *Can a person really make justice, equality, and dignity grow, too?* she wondered. *How?*

Pastor Daniels kept speaking. "In honor of all those hopeful souls who first sat watch for their freedom so long ago, now is the time for every one of us to use this gift we receive tonight. I want each of you to pick one thing you can work on, just one thing you can change for the better, right here in our community."

Murmurs rippled through the congregation. Melody saw Lila scribbling notes on a corner of her program.

"I want you to give this idea some serious thought," Pastor Daniels said. "But don't take too long. When Reverend Dr. King visited with us here in Detroit last summer, he said, '*Now* is the time to lift our nation.' Now is the time, New Hope, for us to lift *our* nation. Now is the time for you"—he pointed one way—"and you"—he pointed the other way—"and you! To take action!"

Melody was sure he was looking directly at her. She held her breath.

"The new year, 1964, is a season of change. Change yourself. Change our community. Change our nation!"

Miss Dorothy, who directed Melody and her friends in the children's choir, began to play the piano. The adult choir rose and began to sing. Melody sang along, clapping in time with the rhythm.

> *We've come this far by faith,*
> *Leaning on the Lord,*
> *Trusting in His holy word,*
> *He's never failed me yet.*
> *Oh, oh, oh, can't turn around,*
> *We've come this far by faith.*

At the conclusion of the song, to Melody's surprise and delight, the church bells sounded, drowning out the final piano notes. It was midnight! It was 1964!

"Happy New Year!" Pastor Daniels shouted.

"Happy Birthday, Melody!" Val shouted, too, squeezing Melody in a hug. But in the din of bells and cheers and applause, only Melody heard.

The Watch Night celebration continued downstairs in the church hall, where everyone greeted each other saying "Happy New Year!" Melody, Val, and Lila stood in line with Yvonne to get cookies, while the rest of the family found seats at one of the tables. Melody tried to spot her best friend, Sharon, in the crowd, but the room was packed.

"There's Diane," Val said.

Melody saw her friend Diane Harris helping her little sisters carry cups of punch. Across the hall Melody saw Miss Esther Collins sitting with a group of other elderly people. Miss Esther was a neighbor who loved gardening just as much as Melody did. She looked up and waved. Melody smiled and waved back.

♪ Watch Night ♪

Yvonne nudged Melody when the lady behind them commented on how pretty the amaryllis flowers were.

"Were they Poppa's idea, or yours?" Yvonne asked.

"Poppa's. But it was my idea to tie the gold ribbons around each pot," Melody said proudly.

Yvonne nodded. "They match your dress,"

"Hey, she's right," Val said.

Melody grinned and tried not to yawn. She didn't want anyone to think she was still too young to be at Watch Night.

With cookies stacked on napkins, Yvonne led them back to a table in the corner where everyone else was sitting. There weren't enough chairs, so Melody sat on Big Momma's lap. She hadn't done that in a while, and tonight something felt different—either Big Momma's lap was getting smaller, or Melody was getting bigger. *Well, I am double digits,* she thought.

"Everyone is talking about the decorations," Yvonne said, passing around the cookies. "And Pastor Daniels's Challenge to Change. I think this thing is going to be big!"

Daddy nodded at her. "'Challenge to Change.' I like that, Yvonne. You know, sometimes when people listen to the news, they think all the change in the way black people are treated only needs to happen down South. But there's plenty of change work to do here in the North, too."

"You're right about that, Will," Val's father, Charles, said.

"Yes," Val's mother, Tish, said, "like the fact that decent, hardworking people can't get a real estate agent to show them certain houses just because they're black!" Tish sounded angry. Although she owned her own hair salon and Charles had a good job as a pharmacist, they were having trouble buying a house.

"You two aren't the only ones facing that battle," Melody's mother said. "Come to our next Block Club meeting. Someone from the Fair Housing Practices Committee is coming to talk to us."

"Is that so?" Charles said.

"We'll be there," Tish said.

"Housing laws need to change," Melody's mother agreed. "But Pastor Daniels asked us to change ourselves, too. I think I might start tutoring after school again."

Yvonne nodded. "I'm going to take Pastor Daniels's

challenge with me when I go back to school. I'm not sure what I'll do on campus, but I know what I can do in the community—well, a community in Mississippi. There's talk about students going there this summer for a civil rights project. I want to go."

Melody's mother shifted in her seat. "What exactly would you all be doing?" she asked.

"A bunch of things. I heard there will be more voter registration, and volunteers will talk to black folks to remind them that they have a say in how this country works. I think they'll also be setting up community centers and schools. I might try working with kids." Yvonne was speaking fast, the way she did when she was excited about an idea.

"Teaching?" Melody asked. "Just like Mommy!" Melody looked at their mother, who looked pleased.

"I thought you were studying business," pointed out Lila, who liked to get all the facts straight.

Yvonne laughed. "I am, Lila. But let's just say that I want to make it my business to help teach black history. Schools are really poor down there. Lots of kids in black communities don't know about the contributions black Americans have made."

"You mean, like Dr. King?" Melody asked.

"And many others," Big Momma said. "Harriet Tubman, Frederick Douglass, and Mrs. Rosa Parks."

"Yes, yes!" Yvonne was bouncing in her seat. "I think when you know about your history, and when you're proud of it, it makes you stronger."

"We sent you to college to learn," Melody's father said, looking steadily at Yvonne.

Daddy paused, and Melody saw Yvonne take a deep breath.

"Seems like you *are* learning," Daddy continued. "To follow your own mind, and make justice and equality grow."

Yvonne let out the breath she'd been holding and smiled. "Thanks, Dad."

"However," Daddy said, leaning forward so that his arms rested on the table, "I want you to be careful in Mississippi and to be safe."

Yvonne laughed. "I know, Dad." But when Daddy gave her a stern look, Yvonne said, "Yes, sir."

Melody smiled, hoping she could have just as much courage in her choice for change as her brave big sister.

"What about you chicks?" Big Momma said to

Melody and Val. "What are you going to do with your gift?"

"Us?" Val replied. "Did Pastor Daniels mean kids, too?"

"Of course he meant kids, too," Melody said excitedly.

"He certainly did," Big Momma said as the grown-ups around the table nodded and smiled.

Suddenly, Yvonne slipped her arm around Melody's shoulder. "Speaking of gifts, somebody should be thinking about her birthday gifts."

"That's right!" Lila slapped the table with her hand. "Dee-Dee is officially ten years old!"

"I am," Melody said, realizing that she'd just stayed awake past midnight for the first time ever. The New Year had begun, and it was her birthday. As she blinked away sleep, she thought about Pastor Daniels's challenge and wondered what great big idea would come her way.

Double-Digits Birthday

On the afternoon on New Year's Day, Melody sorted through the neat stack of records in the living room to find just the right music for her birthday celebration. As she flipped past names she'd heard on the radio or seen on TV, she imagined one day picking up a record with Dwayne's name on it. *Today would be absolutely perfect if only he were here, too,* she thought.

Melody was only halfway through the stack when the doorbell rang.

"Happy Birthday to yooouuu!" Sharon and Diane sang as Melody opened the door.

"Are we too early?" Sharon asked, peeling off her coat and hanging it on one of the hooks by the door. "My dad wanted to drop us off before his football game came on."

"My daddy's upstairs right now listening to a game on the radio," Melody laughed. "And you're right on time."

"What're you doing?" Diane asked, hanging her jacket over Sharon's. She gave Melody a tube-shaped package tied with yarn at either end. It looked like a big piece of candy.

Melody put the package on the coffee table and motioned toward the record player. "I'm trying to find some music."

"Wouldn't it be great if your brother and his group could be here to sing?" Sharon asked.

"Yeah! A live concert would be so cool!" Diane said.

"It would," Melody nodded. "But The Three Ravens aren't in Detroit. They sang at a New Year's concert somewhere in Ohio last night."

"Too bad," Sharon said, sorting through the records lying on the sofa. "Hey! Here's Little Stevie Wonder's 'Fingertips.'" Melody put the record on the turntable and carefully moved the needle arm to its edge.

"*This* is birthday music!" Sharon hopped up, and the girls began to dance.

Sharon was right. The sounds of the harmonica and

Stevie Wonder's 12-year-old voice made Melody want
to move, laugh, celebrate, and sing. They danced their
way across the floor and into the dining room.

Melody barely dodged the kitchen door as her
mother opened it, carrying the triple-chocolate cake on
a blue glass plate.

"Whoa, there, birthday girl!" Mrs. Ellison said,
placing the cake safely in the center of the table.
Melody stopped. Sharon and Diane froze.

"Sorry, Mommy!" Melody said, still bopping her
head to the music.

"Sorry, Mrs. Ellison!" Diane chimed in.

"Me, too!" Sharon said.

Melody's mother gave them a hard look, but then
smiled and shook her shoulders and bopped her head
a few beats, too. Sharon burst out laughing.

Mrs. Ellison shrugged. "Who can keep still when
it's Little Stevie Wonder?" she asked.

As if the music had stirred the entire house into
movement, all at once Daddy, Yvonne, and Lila trooped
downstairs. Then there was a knock at the front door,
and at the same time the telephone rang and someone
was coming into the kitchen from the back door.

♪ Double-Digits Birthday ♪

Mommy went into the kitchen to answer the phone as Yvonne answered the front door. In came Melody's grandparents and her cousins. In the blink of an eye, the dining room was filled with people. Melody didn't know which way to turn first.

"Happy Birthday, chick!" Big Momma was first to give Melody a hug.

"Big Ten!" Cousin Charles said. "Congratulations!"

"Happy Birthday, baby." Cousin Tish gave Melody a kiss. "Love that hairstyle!" she whispered, fluffing Melody's curled bangs. Val, peeking from behind her mother, rolled her eyes and grinned. When she stepped forward, Melody saw that she was holding a small box with a bow on it.

"This is for you," Val said. "Happy, Happy!"

"Gee! I forgot your present!" Sharon said, rushing to the hooks by the front door to dig into her coat pocket. She came back with a soft, tissue-paper-wrapped package. "Sorry, it got a little squished," she said.

Melody didn't care. She was so pleased to have all—nearly all—of her family and friends together on her special day that everything felt pretty wonderful.

"How about we get some candles for this cake and

celebrate our birthday girl?" Melody's father rubbed his hands together and winked at her. He loved Mommy's triple-chocolate cake just as much as Melody did.

"Here we go!" Yvonne placed ten tiny blue candles atop the chocolate frosting in a circle, and another in the middle.

"To grow on," she laughed.

"Ready to sing, everybody?" Lila pulled Melody to stand right in front of her cake, and Daddy lit the candles.

"Where's Mommy?" Melody looked over her shoulder.

"Here!" Her mother stepped in from the kitchen, breathless.

"Happy Birthday to you. Happy Birthday to you. Happy Birthday, dear Melody. Happy birthday to you!"

Melody was beaming. She loved when her family sang together—it was almost like they had their own choir, the way all their voices blended and harmonized in just the right ways! She took a breath but didn't blow out the candles yet. In her family, there was one more verse of the birthday song to sing. Melody smiled and looked around at all their faces, waiting. Suddenly, a solo voice came from the kitchen. It was a high tenor, almost like Smokey Robinson's.

"How o-old are you? How o-old are you? My kid sister, Dee-Dee . . ."

"Dwayne!" Melody squealed, throwing open the kitchen door.

"How o-old are you?" Dwayne finished singing and gave her a bear hug. "Didn't I tell you when I left that I'd show up when you didn't expect it? Happy Birthday!"

Melody pulled Dwayne into the room.

"Well, I declare!" Tish laughed.

"When did you get here?" Lila asked.

Melody noticed that the only people who didn't seem surprised were her mother and father.

"Parents know how to keep secrets, too," Daddy said. "And it was a good one, wasn't it?"

"The best ever!" Melody agreed. Since Dwayne had started working for Motown, he was rarely at home. And when his singing group did come back to town, he spent more time at the studio and at his bandmate Phil's house than he did with the family. Their father wasn't very happy about that, but now they were both smiling, and Melody was glad her birthday had brought them together.

"Let's cut this cake. I'm starved!" Dwayne said. He turned to Melody and gave her a bow. "Birthday girls first, of course."

Melody sat on the floor between Diane and Val with her paper party plate balanced on her knees. Everyone was listening to her brother's stories about traveling around the country with the famous Motown singers. He was telling how he'd accidentally almost tripped one of The Supremes backstage when Val nudged Melody with an elbow.

"When are you going to open your presents?" she whispered, not very quietly.

Dwayne stopped mid-sentence. "Val, they call that a 'stage whisper,'" he laughed, "because the audience is supposed to hear it, too."

Val ducked her head in embarrassment. "Sorry, Dwayne!"

Charles shook his head. "I believe our Valerie likes watching other folks open presents as much as she likes opening presents herself!"

Val had already scrambled up to get Melody's gifts and cards, bringing them to her.

"Open mine first," Sharon said eagerly.

"No, wait." Dwayne went back into the kitchen and came out carrying a record album. "I didn't exactly have time to wrap it," he told his sister.

Melody looked carefully at the bright red cover, and the three young black women looking over their shoulders in the picture. Big orange letters announced the album's artists, Martha and The Vandellas. The album was called *Heat Wave*. That was the name of one of Melody's favorite songs.

Scrawled across the lower corner was a handwritten message. Melody read it out loud: "*Happy Birthday, Dee-Dee. Stay Cool. Martha.*" Melody's mouth dropped open.

Sharon, Val, and Lila crowded around to see.

"Wow, Dwayne! Martha Reeves is one of the hottest stars at Motown right now," Yvonne said. "She's world famous!"

Melody looked at Dwayne. "You got Martha Reeves to autograph it for *me*?" she asked.

Dwayne shrugged and nodded, but he looked pleased that Melody liked her gift.

"Do you really know her?" Sharon asked, starstruck.

"Sort of," he said. "I mean, we're at the studio at the same time . . . sometimes."

"Thank you, Dwayne," Melody said. "You're the best brother ever."

"That's something special," Big Momma said. As Melody passed the album to her grandmother, she saw her father squinting at it.

"How long before we see your face on something like this?" Daddy asked, looking over at Dwayne. Melody shot a look at her brother.

"Dad, I know I have a long way to go. I'm working real hard at it. I'm hoping to get into the studio to record my own music soon."

"I know you'll be just as famous as Martha Reeves one day," Melody said confidently. But Daddy just shook his head.

Melody picked up Sharon's gift. She didn't waste any time unwrapping carefully, the way her sisters did. She tore everything open. The tissue paper ripped away easily, and a length of shiny purple satin ribbon fell into Melody's lap.

"It's for Matching Mondays," Sharon said. "My mom says purple is really hard to find, but she got enough for both of us."

"I love it!" Melody said. Almost every Monday since she and Sharon had met in kindergarten they'd worn the same color hair ribbons to school. Melody carefully wound the ribbon into neat loops. "I got a purple plaid skirt for Christmas," she told Sharon. "This ribbon will go with it perfectly."

Melody was curious about the tube-shaped gift from Diane. When she pulled the paper off, she discovered a tin kaleidoscope. "Neat," she said, holding one end up to her eye and twisting the other end. A colorful burst of patterns shifted inside the tube. "Thanks, Diane."

Next was Val's small box. Inside was a bright new set of jacks and a tiny rubber ball to go with them. "I know you lost one of your other set," Val said.

"I did." Melody gave the ball a quick test bounce, and it flew right into Yvonne's Afro. "Oops!" Melody made a sheepish face. Yvonne simply pulled the ball out, patted her hair back into place, and smiled.

"No ball bouncing indoors!" Daddy said sternly, scooping the ball away from Yvonne. Then he reached to drop it back into its box, which Melody shut quickly. She moved on to her parents' gift, which was wrapped in Christmas paper. It was heavier than she expected. *What could it be?* she wondered.

"Be careful there," Daddy warned. Melody slipped one finger under the lid and popped it off. Inside, nested in crumpled newspapers, was a green transistor radio.

"Ohhh!" she sighed. "My very own radio. Now I can play the music stations I like whenever I want! Thank you, thank you!" Melody immediately turned the radio on and began turning the dial to tune in a station.

Dwayne snapped his fingers when music began to play. "Isn't this a dancing party?" He reached for Melody's hand and pulled her up from the floor. "Come on, Dee-Dee Double Digits. Let's dance!"

Melody followed Dwayne's smooth steps toward the dining room where the floor was clear. In seconds, Charles had gotten Tish up, Lila and Yvonne were moving to the beat, and Val and Sharon were doing a silly bird-like step.

"Are you back to stay? Did you write any new songs? When are you going to make your own record?" Melody asked Dwayne all at once.

"So many questions!" he laughed. "Am I on a quiz show?"

"No," Melody answered. "I missed you, that's all."

"In that case, we're in town for a few weeks to sing backup for some folks and work on a new song I wrote."

"How does it go?"

Dwayne sang:

> *Girl, it's time that I move,*
> *Time for movin' on up.*
> *Yeah, it's time for my move,*
> *Time to start changing my luck.*

"Oh, that sounds good," Melody said. "I like it."

"I do, too," Dwayne told her. "I think it could be a hit. When we get studio time, I want you to sing it with me. I'm not kidding!"

"I know," Melody answered. "I'll do it." But right now she couldn't imagine anything better than this wonderful moment.

Dwayne took her by one hand and spun her around. She almost felt as if she were flying. Everyone was laughing. Her grandparents were clapping. She looked over her shoulder and saw her mother and father dancing, too. She closed her eyes to take a picture with her mind. She felt happy. She felt strong, as if she could do anything.

Later that evening, Melody lay across her bed holding her radio, but it wasn't on. She was listening to her brother and sisters arguing and then laughing down in the living room, the same way they always had. She was smiling when her parents stuck their heads into her room.

"The idea was that you would listen to the radio," her father teased, "not to your squabbling siblings."

"I know, Daddy," Melody laughed. She sat up as Mommy came into the room.

Her mother waved a package. "One more gift!"

Melody could tell from the shape that it was a book. Even though her mother was a math teacher, she loved to read. And she always encouraged other people—especially her children—to love reading, too.

Mommy sat on the edge of her bed. Daddy leaned against the doorway. Melody untied the ribbon and peeled away the paper. "*The First Book of Rhythms*, by Langston Hughes," she read.

As long as she could remember, Melody had heard her father reading aloud poems written by the famous black author. He could even recite some Langston Hughes poems from memory. Sometimes, the poems sounded like music.

Melody flipped through her new book, suprised to see that it wasn't poetry. It was about finding rhythms in poetry and music and even nature. She couldn't wait to read it.

"I saw in the newspaper that Mr. Hughes is going to make an appearance at Hudson's department store in February," Mommy told her.

"Can we go?" Melody asked excitedly.

Mommy nodded.

Melody had started paging through the book again

when a yawn snuck up on her. "I think Melody needs to listen to the rhythm of her sleep," Daddy laughed.

Melody set the book and the radio on the shelf behind her bed and crawled under the covers. Mommy tucked her in, and Daddy kissed her on the forehead. "'Night, my ten-year-old girl."

"'Night, Daddy," Melody murmured. "'Night, Mommy." Her parents went across the hall to their room, and their voices mingled with Lila's, Yvonne's, and Dwayne's. Melody fell asleep listening to the rhythm of her family.

Challenges

t the end of the first week back at school, Melody decided that doing long division and writing compositions weren't quite as interesting as Christmas, Watch Night, or her birthday. She was having trouble staying awake. Big Momma said her body was playing catch-up for all the sleep it had lost while Melody was having fun. On Friday afternoon, Melody blinked as Mrs. Butler rapped on the edge of her desk with a ruler and told the class that she had a special announcement.

"I know it's hard to get back to our schoolwork after having so much free time. But here's something we can all look forward to." She unrolled a poster and tacked it onto the bulletin board.

Melody recognized the face of Frederick Douglass from a book at her grandparents' house, and she remembered his amazing life story: He was born a slave but taught himself to read and write when he was only a boy. He later escaped from slavery, and grew up to travel free all over the world to speak against it. Melody's grandfather said Frederick Douglass's story had always given him the courage to fight for civil rights.

"Our entire school will be celebrating Negro History Week next month," Mrs. Butler said. "We'll have a big assembly, and every class will participate. You can recite a poem, act out a skit, sing, or even present artwork. Which class will do the best job?"

"We will!" Melody chanted with the rest of the class. Melody remembered what Yvonne had said about being proud of what black Americans have contributed to history, and suddenly she had an idea. She pumped her hand into the air.

"Can I make a banner?" she asked when Mrs. Butler called on her.

Mrs. Butler gave her an approving nod. Other kids were eagerly raising their hands. Mrs. Butler began to write their ideas on the chalkboard.

Diane Harris stood up. "Could I sing?" she asked.

"That would be very nice, Diane," Mrs. Butler said.

Diane sat down, leaning across the aisle to Melody. "Will you sing with me?" she whispered.

Melody was flattered. Diane was one of the best singers in their children's choir at church, and she usually sang solos. "I—I guess so," Melody answered sheepishly. Unlike Dwayne, Melody didn't like the attention of standing alone in front of a crowd. She preferred to be one of many voices in a chorus. But singing with Diane at a school assembly would be fun.

"Can I help with your banner?" Sharon asked from her desk on Melody's other side. "My dad can get us a long roll of paper."

Melody nodded. Sharon was good at drawing. "I want to make a banner that includes the names of great people from black history," Melody said.

"We can have important events on it, too," Sharon suggested.

"Great idea," Melody smiled. She couldn't wait to write to Yvonne at college to tell her about the project.

After school, Melody and Sharon waited for Val to

walk the few blocks from her junior high so that they could all walk home together. Lila usually walked with her, but she was staying at school for a meeting of the science club.

"Have you guys thought any more about what Pastor Daniels said on Watch Night?" Melody asked as the girls trudged through the snow. Five inches had fallen while they were in school, and most of the sidewalks were still covered.

"Yeah," Sharon said. "I was thinking I could help out more around the house."

Melody laughed and shook her head. "That doesn't count! He talked about making things better in our *community*." She turned to Val. "Isn't that what he said?"

Val didn't answer. She was looking at her feet. At first, Melody thought it was because of the snow. Val had told them that it almost never snowed in Birmingham. In fact, Val had never needed a winter coat or mittens or boots before she'd moved to Detroit.

Melody tilted her head to see her cousin's face. Val's silence wasn't about the snow. "What's wrong?" Melody asked.

"How can I make a difference in my community when I don't even have one yet?" Val asked, her voice shaking. It sounded like she was trying not to cry.

"Come on, don't say that," Sharon said. "You're a part of *our* community."

"How can I be?" Val said as the girls stopped at Sharon's corner. "We don't even have a house of our own."

Sharon gave Val's arm a reassuring squeeze, said good-bye, and ran the rest of the way home, her boots stomping through the snow.

"Does she always run?" Val asked, watching in amazement.

"Yep," Melody replied. "Ever since kindergarten." But she was thinking about what Val had said. When Val had moved to Detroit eight months earlier, Melody had wanted to help her feel at home. Melody still wanted to help.

"You've got to keep your hopes up," Melody told Val. "Think about the garden I'm going to help you plant at your new house. Think about your own room and painting it any color you want. Your daddy promised, remember?"

Val sighed. "I remember. I just didn't think it would be this hard to find a house."

"Big Momma says, 'Things worth having . . .'"

"Don't come easily," Val finished. "I know."

Melody scooped up a pile of snow in her mitten-covered hands and packed it into a snowball. "Sharon's right," she said. "You don't have to have your own house to be part of the community. You still belong."

Val was silent as they walked the rest of the way to Big Momma and Poppa's house. Melody tossed the snowball from one hand to the other.

As they climbed the snowy steps to the front door, Val said, "I'm in the church choir with you already. I heard some kids talking about a drama club at my school. Maybe I could be part of that. I kind of like that stuff."

"Like plays and musicals?" Melody was excited for her cousin. "Go for it!"

Val smiled. "I think I will. And I'll keep hoping for my bubble-gum-pink bedroom, too."

Melody laughed. "Good," she said brightly, tossing her snowball into the front yard. "Now, don't you hope Big Momma has some of those oatmeal raisin cookies left?"

The Block Club

The following Friday evening, Melody and Lila helped their mother tidy up while Dwayne brought up folding chairs from the basement. The Ellisons were hosting a meeting of the Block Club.

Once a month, several families from the neighborhood got together. The kids played games while their parents talked about what was going on in Detroit and in their community.

"How many chairs do you need, Mom?" Dwayne asked, brushing dust off his pants.

"Four should be enough, with the dining room chairs," their mother said, plumping up the sofa cushions.

Melody stopped stacking Daddy's newspapers for a moment and looked at her brother, remembering last summer, when he had worked at the auto factory after graduating from high school. He'd come home from his shift dirty then, too. Now he was almost always neat and clean and had a fresh haircut. She giggled.

"What?" Dwayne smiled.

"Nothing. It's just so great that you're at home for a while," she said.

"Home?" Lila shook her dusting rag in Dwayne's direction. "He's never at home. He's always over at Motown, acting like singing is real work."

"Sure it is! We don't just sing. We have classes on how to dress up, how to talk if we get interviewed by reporters, even how to eat in a fancy restaurant. And . . ." Dwayne spun in one of the new moves that he'd learned. "We get dance lessons from a real choreographer."

Mommy was nodding her approval. "Mr. Berry Gordy must care a lot about how his performers behave," she said.

"Yes, he does," Dwayne said.

Lila shrugged and kept dusting.

Dwayne snapped his fingers in her direction. "If you feel like that, Lila, I guess you don't want an invite to see Hitsville U.S.A. up close, and get a tour of the Motown studio, huh?"

Lila froze. "Wh-what?"

"I do! I do!" Melody shouted.

"So do I," Mommy said.

"I'll see what I can do," Dwayne answered. Melody thought he sounded very important.

Dwayne looked at his watch. "Speaking of the studio, I gotta run. The Three Ravens are doing backup for a new singer. Bye!"

Melody's mother had a funny look on her face as Dwayne pecked her on the cheek and rushed away. After he left, Mommy shook her head. "I do wish Dwayne were going to college," she said, almost to herself. "Still, he's turning into quite a young man."

"Does Daddy think so?" Lila asked.

Melody was wondering the same thing.

"Your father is proud of all of you," Mommy said firmly. "Let's get the sandwiches made. People will start showing up in less than an hour!"

They were all heading to the kitchen when the doorbell rang. "I'll get it," Melody said, wondering who was arriving so early.

"Miss Esther!" Melody said when she opened the door. "Come in."

"I know I'm early for the meeting," Miss Esther said, tapping her way into the living room with her cane. "But I have something for you."

Melody took Miss Esther's coat and hat. The scent of gardenias from Miss Esther's perfume filled the air. It reminded Melody of summer. "Please sit down," Melody said, using her best company manners. But Miss Esther didn't really feel like company. She felt like family.

"I'm so sorry I missed your birthday celebration," Miss Esther said. She sat on the sofa with her big brown purse upright on her lap. "So tonight I came before the others to give you a belated gift." She opened the purse with a loud snap, and took out two small burlap pouches that were no larger than Melody's hands. One had a red drawstring cord, the other a green one.

"Thank you," Melody said, sitting down on the sofa. She peeked inside the red-corded pouch. "Seeds!" She smiled up at Miss Esther. "What kind are they?"

"Those are hollyhocks, and they're very special. They're called 'heirlooms.' They grow from seeds that are collected from plants every year and passed on from generation to generation."

Melody's face lit up. Poppa had taught her about heirloom plants. He'd taken her many times to the botanical gardens at Belle Isle Park. He said some of the plants came from seeds that were a hundred years old. "My grandfather calls heirloom plants 'great-great-grandflowers,'" Melody said.

"Is that right?" Miss Esther laughed.

"Oh, I can't wait to plant these," Melody said.

"They'll grow almost as tall as you are," Miss Esther said. "I brought them up from my mother's garden in Alabama when I first came to Detroit as a young woman. I had a big, beautiful garden at my first home here in the city. Now I don't have the space—or the energy—for one."

Melody wanted to ask lots of questions, like where in Alabama Miss Esther came from, and what kind of garden she had, and what her other Detroit house had looked like. But before she could say anything, Miss Esther pointed to the other pouch.

"That's a type of bean. It's called Good Mother Stallard."

Melody laughed. "That's a funny name for a bean! Is it an heirloom, too?" She poured a few of the seeds into her palm to look at them more closely.

"Yes, it is." Miss Esther sat back and smiled. "Did you know that planting is one of the traditions we keep from some of our African ancestors? Thousands of years ago they were growing beans—and okra and squash, and yams."

"Yams came from Africa?" Melody thought of the yams Big Momma baked at Thanksgiving. "No, ma'am. I didn't know," Melody said, admiring the pretty maroon-and-white beans. Was it her imagination that they seemed to tingle in her hand?

"Well, gardening is a very good thing to carry on. I knew I'd picked the right young person to hand these heirlooms down to. We can talk more about how and where to plant them another time, all right?"

"Yes, ma'am," Melody said, putting the seeds back in the pouch. Miss Esther's confidence in her made Melody feel special. It reminded her of the conversation with Yvonne on New Year's Eve when Yvonne had said that Melody was a responsible person.

Right then Melody's mother came out of the kitchen

holding a plate piled with triangle-shaped sandwiches. "Hello, Miss Esther! How are you this evening?"

"I am well, thank you, Frances," Miss Esther said. "Melody and I have been discussing gardening."

While her mother and Miss Esther chatted, Melody went upstairs to put the burlap pouches away in her dresser drawer. Across the hall, Melody heard her father getting up from his after-work nap. Downstairs the doorbell sounded, and she heard people's voices greeting one another as they came in. Melody grabbed her pack of Old Maid playing cards and headed down.

The living room was crowded with familiar faces, and Melody politely said hello to each adult. There was Sharon's mother, and Diane's parents, and the parents of Julius Sterling, a boy from school. Val's father and mother were there, too. They were standing right in front of the kitchen door talking with Julius's father, and they didn't notice Melody waiting to pass. They all wore serious expressions.

"I'm glad you came tonight," Mr. Sterling said to Charles and Tish.

Charles nodded. "You know, in Birmingham there were plenty of neighborhoods where Negroes weren't welcome to live. But I didn't think we'd find housing discrimination so bad in Detroit."

"That's one of the reasons we marched in the Walk to Freedom last summer," Mr. Sterling said. "Tonight's speaker is from the Greater Detroit Committee for Fair Housing Practices. That group works with black families wanting to buy homes in certain neighborhoods. They find white families who are willing to sell to them, no matter how their neighbors feel about it."

"We didn't move from Alabama to be told what Negroes can or can't do because of the color of their skin," Tish said. "That's not American!"

Charles nodded. "We love staying with my Uncle Frank and Aunt Geneva," he explained to Mr. Sterling. "But my wife and daughter have their hearts set on us being in our own home by spring, and I'm ready to do whatever it takes to make that happen!"

"I'll take you over to meet our speaker," Mr. Sterling said. When the grown-ups moved toward the living room, Melody was able to get into the kitchen. Val, Sharon, and Diane were sitting at the table, munching on popcorn.

Julius was there, too. "Hey, Melody!" he said.

Melody liked Julius a lot. He didn't seem to care whether he was around boys or girls. He told jokes and talked baseball just the same.

"Hi, everybody. Hey back, Julius." Melody said. She turned on the radio that her mother kept on the counter beside the refrigerator.

"This meeting is going to be boring," Diane said, folding her arms across her chest.

"Maybe not," Melody said, glancing at Val. Val raised her eyebrows, as if to ask, "What is it?" But Melody couldn't tell her. Big Momma always said families shouldn't discuss their private business in front of people who *weren't* family.

"Well, anyway, we don't have to be bored," Melody said. "I brought my Old Maid cards."

Sharon waved her bingo game in the air, but Julius plunked a box on the table.

"Dominoes." He looked around at all the girls. "Anybody know how to play?"

"I do," Sharon said.

"Me, too," Val said, nodding. "My daddy showed me."

Diane unfolded her arms and relaxed. "I do, too.

My granddad taught me," she said. "I'll play!"

Melody shrugged and laughed. "I guess I'm the only one who doesn't know."

"That's okay. I'll show you," Julius said. "It's a lot of fun."

Melody sat down. Two games and one big bowl of popcorn later, everyone was having a good time, and Melody had put all the talk of fair housing out of her mind. As Diane was adding up the score, the adult voices in the other room got louder. The kids stopped their own conversation to listen. Melody got up from her chair and went to ease the door open a crack.

"I tell you, we need to do something about the new management at Fieldston's Clothing Store," someone said. "They're right here in a Negro community, but they act as if every Negro customer is there to steal something!"

"That's not right," Melody's father said. "Old Mr. Fieldston never would have stood for that when he was alive."

Melody thought about what had happened to her and Dwayne. Without thinking, she opened the door wide and barged into the living room.

"Fieldston's *does* discriminate against black people!" she said, walking into the middle of the circle of chairs.

All eyes turned toward Melody, including her parents' and Miss Esther's.

"And how do you know that?" Diane's mother asked, surprised.

As that day with Dwayne flashed in her memory, Melody got angry again. "I know because the manager accused me of shoplifting," she said.

"Say what?" Her father half rose from his chair. Mommy put a hand on his arm.

"When was this?" Mommy asked.

"It was last spring. I went to help Dwayne pick out a suit," Melody said. "Dwayne was just trying on a jacket, and the manager made him take it off. Then he started yelling and made us leave the store before we could buy anything. I don't think we should spend our money in a store that treats us like that."

Julius's father was nodding. "My butcher shop is just a few doors up from Fieldston's, and I hear the same story over and over. I think we ought to protest by boycotting Fieldston's."

"You mean not shop there at all?" Mrs. Harris said.

"Yes," Melody's father answered. "And I say we picket in front of the store, too. We can hand out leaflets that explain how they treat black customers. They may not want to notice us, but they notice our money. And they'll notice when it's gone."

Melody's stomach felt trembly as she thought of the TV news reports of black and white people protesting against racial discrimination. Sometimes there were police, and the protesters got arrested.

"You're talking carrying signs?" Charles asked.

Miss Esther cleared her throat. "I don't see why not. We should speak up with our voices," she said, giving Melody an approving look. "And with our pocketbooks."

Miss Esther's comment made Melody realize that some of the other adults thought she should be quiet. But she couldn't. She turned to her mother. "Mommy, you told me that what we do with our money says a lot about what we believe."

"I did say that," her mother said. "Thank you for reminding me, Melody. I think we should consider Miss Esther's and Mr. Sterling's suggestions." She glanced around the room. "Melody, I think that concludes your part of the meeting," she said gently.

There was a buzz of reaction as Melody left the room. The kitchen door was wide open, and all her friends were bunched there staring at her.

"Oh, my goodness!" Val dragged Melody into the kitchen. "I can't believe you went out there and interrupted the meeting."

Melody thought of Yvonne, who always told her to use her voice and speak up about fairness. She knew Yvonne would be pleased.

"Do you really think people will boycott Fieldston's?" Diane asked. "My mom shops there all the time."

"She won't be able to if there's a picket line in front of the store," Julius said.

"I saw picket lines in Birmingham," Val said. "People carried signs and marched in front of stores or restaurants that wouldn't serve black people."

All of a sudden, Melody made a decision. "I'm going to make a picket sign, and I'm going to carry it in the boycott. If my parents let me."

"Are you nuts?" Julius asked.

Melody just shook her head. "This is about being

fair. Maybe a boycott will make Fieldston's change. Wouldn't that be better for everybody?"

"Mostly for our parents," Julius said.

"That's not true," Val said. "If our parents don't get treated fairly, we don't either. In Alabama a sign on a water fountain that says 'Whites Only' means grown-ups *and* kids. That's why kids have been standing up and marching for equal rights."

Diane nodded. "Maybe all of us kids should march."

"Yes," Melody said. "And maybe there are other things we could do around here to prove that kids can make things better, too."

After breakfast the next morning, Melody took Bo for a walk. Her brain was busy—she was thinking about the Fieldston's boycott and her Negro History Week banner. Bo tugged at his leash as they passed Sharon's house, but Melody didn't stop, because she knew that Sharon's family liked to sleep late on Saturdays. They did stop across the street from Miss Esther's bright yellow house. Bo barked and sniffed at something underneath the snow.

Melody realized that they were standing outside the community playground. She hadn't played there in ages! Along the chain-link fence, Melody looked for the small sign she remembered, the one that read "Park closes at dusk." But she couldn't find it—a wild tangle of a hedge had grown up almost as tall as the fence. Melody frowned at how messy it looked.

The gate was open, so Melody and Bo went in. It was a Saturday morning and not very cold, but the playground was empty. Melody looked around. There had once been flower beds along the fence, but Melody couldn't remember seeing anything blooming in the park last summer. Now she could see clumps of dead weeds and uncut grass bunched in the snow.

She smiled at the jungle gym, remembering how Yvonne had helped her climb it when she was little. But now the bars were rusting. Melody turned to the swings, remembering Dwayne pushing her and Lila and singing a made-up song:

> *Dee-Dee and Lila flying so high,*
> *Two little sisters touching the sky!*

Now, three of the four swings were missing, and the remaining one was dangling from a broken chain, the seat touching the ground. Some of the bricks were missing from the handball courts, and others were crumbling. The paint on the benches was peeling, and the dented trash can was tipped over. It didn't look like anyone was paying attention to the park.

Melody shook her head. No wonder no one was using it. "This used to be such a fun place to play," she said to Bo. "Somebody should do something."

Bo looked up at her and barked.

"Me?" Melody bent to tickle the spot between Bo's ears. "I don't know . . ." She took another slow walk around the paths, and as she did her brain got busy again. But this time, she was imagining the playground filled with kids having fun. She pictured a shiny new jungle gym, spiffy swings, and tons of beautiful flowers. There could be a vegetable garden, and even a stage for music shows.

Melody felt her heart pounding with excitement. The Fieldston's boycott was important, but fixing up the playground could be her own special way of making things better in her community. "This is it, Bo!"

Melody said. "This is *my* Challenge to Change."

Melody tugged Bo's leash. "Come on," she said. Her big sister was just the person to help her figure out where to start. If she hurried, she'd have enough time to write Yvonne a letter before the mailman came. Melody started to run.

Books and Banners

*W*hen dinner was over on Sunday afternoon, Melody and Val were sprawled on the living room rug, sketching ideas for picket signs for the Fieldston's protest. Big Momma was playing the piano softly behind the girls while the other grown-ups read the Sunday newspaper. Melody hadn't told anyone about her playground plan yet. She thought it would be better to wait and see if Yvonne thought it was a good idea, first.

"Listen to this," Poppa said, crinkling the newspaper pages to get everyone's attention. "It says here that Detroit is planning big doings when that Langston Hughes comes to town in three weeks!"

"Oh!" Melody hopped up. "We're going to see him at Hudson's department store. I hope he'll autograph the book I got for my birthday." She leaned against her grandfather's arm to look at the paper.

Tish nodded. "My clients at the salon have been talking about it. There will be fancy dinners and parties all weekend. On Saturday night there's a big gala dance in Mr. Hughes's honor. I heard the mayor might even give him the key to the city."

"How can a city have a key?" Val asked.

Charles looked at her over the top of the sports pages. "It's really a way to show respect."

Melody's mother nodded. "Sometimes it's not even a real key. The idea is to say to a person, 'You're welcome to visit us anytime. We consider you an honorary citizen of our city.'"

"It's all so exciting. I can't wait!" Melody clapped her hands. "I hope there's a parade, and maybe fireworks."

Melody's father smiled. "I don't think there will be fireworks in February, daughter. But this is a big deal to have our city honor Mr. Hughes—not only because he's a Negro, but because he's a great poet."

Big Momma stopped playing to point to the bookcase in the corner. "Look over there, Melody. We have a volume of his poems."

Melody skipped across the room to the neatly arranged shelves. "Oh, here it is." She reached to take the book out, and her eyes dropped to the shelf below. *"The Pictorial History of the Negro in America,"* she read out loud, and suddenly she thought of the banner she and Sharon were making. "Big Momma, may I borrow this book?" she asked.

"Of course, chick!" Big Momma turned away from the piano keys to give Melody a curious look. "Do you need it for school?"

Melody held the book against her chest with both hands. "Kind of. See, the week after Mr. Hughes comes to town is—"

"Negro History Week!" Val shouted. "Our school is having an assembly, and my class is doing a skit." She smiled at Melody. Val had joined the drama club, and Melody could tell that she was enjoying it.

"So what is your class doing, Melody?" Mommy asked.

"Mrs. Butler let us each decide," Melody explained. "I'm singing a song with Diane, but I'm also making a banner with Sharon. We want to put important people and stuff on it, so everyone can learn black history."

Poppa's newspaper rustled as he clapped while he still held it in his hands. "George Washington Carver!" he shouted. "He did great research with peanuts at Tuskegee, and his work was important to black *and* white farmers!"

"Mary McLeod Bethune, educator," Mommy said.

"Marian Anderson, opera singer!" Big Momma said.

Melody dropped the book on the coffee table and reached for her pencil. "Wait, wait!" she said. "I want to write these names down."

"Charles Drew," Charles called out. "And not because we have the same name!" Everyone laughed. "Seriously. He was a surgeon who figured out how to preserve blood for sick people who needed transfusions."

"Elijah J. McCoy," Daddy said quietly. "Trained as an engineer over a hundred years ago, but couldn't get a job doing that because of his skin color. He went to work on the railroad, and invented a device to help oil move through engines. Lived the last part of his life right here in Detroit."

"Well!" Poppa said, nodding his head. "I learn something every day."

"History is full of strong Negro Americans," Big Momma said, starting to play another piece on the piano. "Many people have heard of leaders like Mrs. Rosa Parks and Dr. King. But there are many less well-known people who have done extraordinary things, too. Your banner is a good idea, chick."

Melody smiled as she started making a list.

By the middle of the week, Melody had two pages full of names and dates. Sharon came to her house after school on Thursday, and they unwound a roll of paper across the kitchen table. Sharon anchored one end with her book bag, and Melody set her radio at the other end and turned it on. She plopped her 64-color crayon box in the center.

Sharon pulled a folded paper from her pocket, and Melody could see Sharon's tiny handwriting scrawled all over its back and front.

Melody looked at her own notes. "I think we might have more names than we have room on the paper," she said.

"Wow," Sharon said, looking at Melody's list.

"Maybe we have some of the same names."

"Let's check that out first," Melody said. She began reading the names on her list, and Sharon started crossing those names off her paper.

Lila popped into the kitchen and grabbed a banana from the fruit bowl. Melody was surprised that she'd taken a break from her books. Lila had passed her exams and won the science scholarship to a private high school. She wouldn't start until the fall, but instead of taking it easy, she seemed to spend even more time studying. Melody believed her sister actually *liked* homework.

"Your friend Diane just pulled up out front," Lila said, looking over Melody's shoulder. She started reading the names aloud. "Joe Louis, Jackie Robinson. No female athletes? What is wrong with you two? Althea Gibson, first black person—man or woman—to win a Grand Slam in tennis!" Lila peeled her banana and marched out of the kitchen.

Melody quickly scribbled down the information as Sharon shook her head. "How does she know that stuff? Does she even play tennis?"

"Nope," Melody answered, and the girls broke into

giggles as the doorbell rang.

Melody got up to answer the door. When she and Diane came back to the kitchen, Diane was explaining that she had just come from her music lesson at Big Momma's.

"Guess what," Diane said, laying her sheet music right on top of the banner paper. "I found the perfect song for us to sing at the assembly."

"What is it?" Melody asked.

"It's a freedom song," Diane said. "'We Shall Overcome.'"

Sharon's face lit up. "What a good idea."

"That's perfect," Melody said, nodding. "Yvonne told me that her friends at college sing freedom songs when they protest against discrimination. They sing to encourage one another. Sometimes they even change the words and sing about the people or businesses they're protesting."

"Your grandma said that freedom songs are part of our past, and that they're an important part of the civil rights movement now," Diane explained. "It's a way to be connected to the people who came before us."

"Just like the people on our banner!" Melody said.

"Oh," Diane said, looking at the paper under her sheet music. "Is that what this is? If it's as good as those signs in your dining room, everybody will be talking about it at the assembly."

Sharon frowned. "What signs?"

"The ones my dad is collecting for the Fieldston's boycott," Melody explained. She shook her head at Diane. "We didn't make those. But when Sharon and I are done, our banner will look great. Right, Sharon?"

"Right," Sharon said.

Langston Hughes Weekend was the second weekend in February. On the morning of the book signing, Melody was too excited to sit still. As Lila combed and braided her hair, Melody held her purple hair ribbons and listened to the news on her transistor radio about Mr. Hughes's arrival at the Detroit airport the day before.

"Wow, there was a motorcade of seven cars!" she said. "What's a motorcade?"

"A parade with cars but no floats or marching bands," Lila said. "Hold still, or your braids will be crooked!"

Melody nodded, forgetting that she was moving. Lila sighed.

"You sisters almost ready?" Dwayne stood in their bedroom doorway, dangling car keys.

Lila dropped the comb she was using. "Don't tell me Mom is letting *you* get behind the wheel! I still can't believe you learned how to drive."

Both the girls had been stunned when Dwayne told them he'd gotten his driver's license. He'd always been too focused on his music to care about much else, including taking the driving test.

"I didn't know you were coming to the book signing, Dwayne," Melody said happily.

"A couple of other Motown singers are supposed to show up at the store, so I thought I would check it out."

"Hmm," Lila mumbled, finishing Melody's hair.

"I can't wait to get my book signed," Melody said. "Maybe I can start an autograph collection. I already have a signed record album. What do you think, Lila?"

"I think we'd better hurry up."

They piled into the car a few minutes later, and Mommy sat in the front passenger seat instead of behind the wheel. Dwayne turned out to be a good

driver. He was almost as smooth at handling a car as
Daddy or Poppa. Melody was fascinated by cars and
driving. She often daydreamed about cruising along
the highway, wearing sunglasses and driving her own
car. Maybe it would be a convertible.

"Remember," Mommy said on the way to the store.
"We're going to use our best manners today."

"Mommy, we're not little kids," Melody said.

When Dwayne pulled up near the Woodward
Avenue entrance to Hudson's, their mother leaned to
check her reflection in the rearview mirror before she
opened the car door.

"I think Mom is starstruck!" Lila whispered.

Melody smiled, but she was distracted. She was
studying the line that had formed along the front of
the store. It was so long! Men, women, and children
were standing in it, and it stretched almost to the
corner. There were old people, young people, people of
many races. Lots of them were carrying books just like
Melody was.

Dwayne went to park the car, and Melody, Lila, and
Mommy went to the end of the line.

Melody couldn't keep still. She clutched her copy of

The First Book of Rhythms closer to her chest, crushing and wrinkling the collar of the crisply ironed blouse she wore underneath her coat. Since her birthday, Melody had read the entire book three times. Now she was going to meet the person who had written it!

After a few minutes, Melody said, "The line's not moving at all."

"Do you think we're going to get in?" Lila asked.

"I'm sure we'll be fine," Mommy said. "Be patient, girls."

Melody stepped out of the line to look for Dwayne. She was amazed at what she saw. The line was getting longer. Hudson's covered an entire block, and now the trail of people stretched around the corner!

Melody joined her mother and sister again. The line crept slowly, reminding Melody of the tortoises at the zoo. Gradually she and her mother and sister passed the last of the huge display windows and walked through the doors. Dwayne came up just in time.

"Sorry, I'm with them," he said to the surprised man he stepped in front of. "Wow, what a turnout! People are treating this man like a rock 'n' roll star, or something."

"He *is* a star," Mommy said in her teacher-in-the-classroom voice. "Langston Hughes is a *literary* star."

"I know, Mom," Dwayne said. He began to quote from one of their father's favorite Langston Hughes poems. *Good morning, daddy! Ain't you heard the boogie-woogie rumble of a dream deferred?"*

Melody was very impressed. "You actually listened when Daddy read that poem?" she asked.

"He didn't read it," Dwayne said. "He knew it by heart. So I memorized it, too."

"Looks like Mr. Hughes is a recording star, too, Dwayne." Lila pointed to the big poster on a stand just outside the book department.

Welcome, Mr. Langston Hughes! Motown Presents: **Poets of the Revolution**, *the first-ever spoken-word recording and collaboration between poets Langston Hughes and Detroit's Margaret Danner! Coming soon from our very own Hitsville U.S.A.*

Dwayne snapped his fingers and began to look around. "So that's why Marvin Gaye and The Supremes are here. Langston Hughes is working with Motown. He's making a poetry album!"

"I've got to write that title down," Mommy said,

rooting around in her purse for a pen and paper.

Melody was eager to hear what Langston Hughes's voice sounded like. She peeked around Lila to see if she could catch sight of the author. Way ahead Melody could see a round-faced man wearing black eyeglasses. He was sitting at a table piled with books. *That must be him!* Melody thought.

A woman beside the table announced that Mr. Hughes was going to read his poem "Youth." Then she adjusted a microphone, and he began to speak.

> *We have tomorrow*
> *Bright before us*
> *Like a flame.*

Melody closed her eyes to listen to the rhythm in the way his words flowed. That's what *The First Book of Rhythms* was all about, how everything—voices speaking, plants growing, the sun's rise and setting—everything had a pattern or rhythm. The poet's soft voice reminded Melody of a musical instrument, and his poem was a song.

Yesterday
A night-gone thing,
A sun-down name.
And dawn-today
Broad arch above
The road we came.

We march!
Americans together,
We march!

Everyone waiting in line broke into applause. Melody looked up at Dwayne, who was clapping hard, too.

When she got to the front of the line, Melody felt shy. Her mother nudged her forward. Melody put her book on the table, unable to say anything. Mr. Hughes smiled and asked how she wanted it signed.

"To Melody Ellison," she said. "Please!" she added. While Mr. Hughes was writing, she tried to think of something else to say. "My daddy knows some of your poems by heart," she finally whispered. "He likes your writing and I do, too!"

Mr. Hughes smiled again and thanked Melody, and then he handed her book back to her. Melody barely remembered to say "Thank you" herself before turning away.

"You were wonderful," her mother said, giving Melody a hug. "Wait until Daddy hears about this. He's so pleased that you love words as much as he does. This will make his day!"

Melody opened her book, and Lila leaned in to see the autographed page. Melody touched the neat script handwriting carefully, so she wouldn't smudge it. She could hardly believe that she had just met and spoken to a real, world-famous literary star.

As they stepped out of the book-signing line, Melody turned around, looking for Dwayne. Her brother was walking toward a man and a woman who had just come into the book department. Melody recognized the man in the suit and tie—that was the singer Marvin Gaye! And next to him was a slim young woman with wide eyes and a fancy hairdo. It was Diana Ross of The Supremes! She stopped talking to Marvin Gaye and looked in Dwayne's direction. She smiled and waved one of her white-gloved hands.

"Girls, did you see that?" Mommy said. "That was one of The Supremes, waving at our Dwayne!"

"That was really neat," Melody said.

Even Lila agreed. "It sure was," she said.

When Dwayne joined his mother and sisters, he acted like it was no big deal that Diana Ross had waved at him. But Melody knew that he was trying hard not to break into a grin.

In the days after the book signing, Melody couldn't get Mr. Hughes's poem out of her head: *"We march! Americans together, we march!"* The words were like a drumbeat. Like feet on pavement. And as she and Sharon were putting the finishing touches on their banner the day before the assembly, those words also reminded Melody of people marching through time.

Sharon had just stretched the banner to its full length across the floor of Melody's living room and into the dining room. They had written the numbers for each year in different colors, starting with 1619, the year the first African slaves had been brought to Plymouth Colony. That year was brown, for the people and for the land they'd left. The banner listed people and places and events, right up to 1964: *Langston Hughes Weekend, Detroit, Michigan.*

"It looks great!" Sharon said.

But Melody shook her head. "Sharon, we have to change the banner."

"What? Do you see a spelling mistake?"

"No . . . I just think it would be perfect if it said, 'We March Through Negro History.'" Melody tried to explain about Mr. Hughes's poem and the marching in her head.

Sharon squinted at the paper and sighed. "Why did you have to come up with such a good idea *now*?" she moaned. "We don't have time to start all over."

"We don't have to," Melody said, picking up a curled tube of leftover paper lying underneath the edge of the sofa. "We could write the headline on this and tape it to the beginning of our time line."

"We could make it look like the title of a book, or something," Sharon said thoughtfully.

"And we can use all the colors for the letters," Melody said.

"Let's do it!"

They worked quickly, finishing just as the telephone rang. Melody's mother answered it in the kitchen. A few minutes later, she came into the dining room.

"Sharon, that was your mother, asking you to head home. Are you two almost done?"

Melody and Sharon got up from their knees as Mommy looked at the banner. "It's beautiful, girls!" Mommy said as she walked along the banner, reading. "This is great work."

"Do you really think so, Mrs. Ellison?" Sharon asked.

"Sharon, if I were giving you a grade on this, it would be an A," Mommy said.

The next morning, Melody, Sharon, and Diane sat together with their class in the school auditorium at the start of second period. Melody and Sharon's banner was on display above the stage. When Mrs. Butler had seen it, she had been so impressed that she had decided to hang it in the auditorium so that everyone could see it.

"Man!" Sharon whispered. "Look at that!"

"And the 'March' part looks like we planned it all along," Melody whispered back.

"Thanks to you," Sharon said.

"No, thanks to you!" Melody said. Mrs. Butler turned from the row in front of them with a warning look, so they stopped talking.

The younger kids went first. With the exception of a very loud little girl, all the first-grade classes sang together. A second-grader bravely got onstage by himself and read an essay about Crispus Attucks, the black man who was the first person to die at the start of the American Revolution, when the American colonies fought to gain their independence from Great Britain.

A third-grade class did a skit about Ida B. Wells Barnett, who had been a black journalist. Her newspaper equipment had been destroyed by people who were angry about the stories she wrote demanding justice and equality for black Americans.

It seemed to take forever until it was time for Melody and Diane to go up on the stage. Finally, Mrs. Butler introduced them. "Now, boys and girls, fourth-graders Melody Ellison and Diane Harris will perform a very special song."

"Do it!" Sharon whispered, as they got up from their seats.

Melody stood at one side of the upright piano with her hands at her sides, facing the audience but with Diane in her side view. Diane sat gracefully on the piano seat and held her hands over the keys. Melody took several deep breaths as she watched Diane play the introduction. Then it was time to sing.

> *We shall overcome,*
> *We shall overcome,*
> *We shall overcome someday.*
> *Oh, deep in my heart, I do believe,*
> *We shall overcome someday.*

Melody wasn't nervous. Seeing Sharon in the audience helped her relax. Melody thought of the banner that was hanging above her and about the names of all the people who had come before her. She sang louder.

From the audience, Melody heard two familiar voices begin to sing along. There, in the back of the auditorium, were Big Momma and Miss Dorothy! They must have decided to come to watch the assembly.

The two had been friends, singing together, for years. Now they were singing with Melody and Diane. Gradually, the rest of the audience joined in until the auditorium was filled with the sound of one great big choir.

> *We'll walk hand in hand,*
> *We'll walk hand in hand,*
> *We'll walk hand in hand, someday.*
> *Oh, deep in my heart, I do believe,*
> *We'll walk hand in hand someday.*

As Melody sang, she thought of all the people whose names were on the banner, and how many of them had overcome hardships and injustice to do great things. She thought of last autumn when she'd overcome her fear and sadness once she decided to sing for the four Birmingham girls. She had walked hand in hand with her closest friends, and overcome everything. Now, singing this freedom song, Melody felt free in a way she hadn't before.

We March!

CHAPTER 7

When Melody got home from school, there was a letter from Yvonne in the mailbox. *Finally!* Melody thought. Yvonne usually wrote back right away, but Mommy had told Melody that Yvonne was especially busy at school.

> *February 11, 1964*
> *Dear Dee-Dee,*
>
> *I'm sorry it took me so long to write back to you. I had to finish a big project for my economics class, and I was helping plan some events for Negro History Week here on campus. But I haven't forgotten about your idea. I'm so proud of you for wanting to clean up the park. I loved going there and playing on the jungle gym with you and Lila*

when you were little. Remember how you loved to go down the slide but were afraid to climb up the ladder? I helped you up the steps, and we sailed down the slide together. I think it's a great answer to the Challenge to Change.

It's a big job, but I bet the other kids in the neighborhood will work with you. It would be fun to do it together. Just ask them. Oh, and don't be afraid to ask for help from a grown-up. Remember what Pastor Daniels said: It's a season of change!

Let me know how things go,
Love, Vonnie

Melody folded the letter. Vonnie supported her idea, just as she'd hoped. She knew her sister was right about asking for help. After tomorrow's protest, Melody would do just that.

At ten o'clock the next morning, a group gathered in front of Julius's father's butcher shop. Even though

it was cold, almost fifty people had shown up to protest. Melody stood in a line with her mother while her
father walked among the people, passing out leaflets
and some of the signs that had been piling up at the
Ellisons' house. Melody had made her own sign. It said,
"Support Our Boycott!" She was ready to hold it up
high and march.

The picketing was to begin at ten-thirty, and by
then the line was even longer. Melody saw Diane and
her parents, and Sharon with her mother. She saw
kids from school, and one or two teachers. Lila was up
ahead, standing with her friends. Melody wished that
Val was there, but Val's parents had taken the morning
off from work to go look at houses, and Val had gone
with them.

"Don't worry if you get tired," Melody heard her
father telling an older member of their church. "We've
got people to relieve you. This protest will go on until
the store closes today, but we'll be back every Saturday
until this store changes the way they treat black
customers!"

Julius's father appeared at the door of his shop, took
off his apron, and handed it to someone inside. Then he

took Julius by the hand and stepped to the front of the line. He bent to pick up a sign.

"Shop in Dignity!" he chanted, walking slowly along the sidewalk.

Melody got a good grip on her sign and began to pick up the chant. At the corner past Fieldston's, the line crossed the street and marched on the other side. People turned their signs so that anyone looking out of the Fieldston's window could read them.

Many of the protesters looked straight ahead when they walked past the Fieldston's window, but Melody couldn't. When she was in front of the store, she turned to stare. She found herself looking right at the same man—the manager—who'd yelled at her and Dwayne. For a second their eyes locked.

Do you recognize me? Melody wondered. Maybe he had falsely accused so many people that he didn't remember her. The man's face grew paler as he real-ized that the line was not ending. The chanting was not stopping. Other clerks moved to the display window. Some looked shocked. One woman looked angry. But they all stood frozen, almost like mannequins.

Melody kept her eyes on the window after she

passed the store. She saw a white man stop at the door. But Melody's father handed the man one of the leaflets. The man read it, and then backed away and left without crossing the picket line.

Black shoppers who passed on the street but were not part of the picket line seemed to have mixed reactions. A few gave them curious looks. Some hurried past, as if they didn't want to be a part of it. Melody thought of Val's father. She knew he supported equal rights, but Charles had said that in Alabama, being part of even a peaceful march or protest could cause a black man to lose his job—or get put in jail. Today there was no trouble, and not a policeman in sight.

Someone began to sing. Melody didn't recognize the voice, but she knew the song. It was the same one the crowd had sung during the Walk to Freedom when Dr. King had been in Detroit. Melody sang along.

> *We shall not,*
> *We shall not be moved.*

The chanting stopped and the singing grew louder.

We shall not,
We shall not be moved.
Just like a tree that's standing by the water,
We shall not be moved.

But then the words changed. Melody hummed along, listening to the part she'd never heard before.

We're fighting for our children,
We shall not be moved.

Melody was at the corner. She looked at the line and guessed there were now at least a hundred people protesting. She saw a young man, wearing a hat pulled low, ease between two of the marchers. It was Dwayne!

Melody was surprised. Last year, Dwayne had refused to go with the family to the Walk to Freedom. He'd said that he didn't think marches could change anything and that becoming a rich and famous singer was what would make people treat him fairly. But Melody knew, from the letters he'd sent home while he was touring, that Dwayne had changed his mind. He had told her that even the Motown stars were treated unfairly at some hotels and restaurants. *Seems like our talent is colored first, and great second,* he had written.

Now her brother spotted her. Their eyes met and held for a moment. Then Dwayne shook his head. Melody understood that he didn't want her to tell anyone he was there. Melody pinched her thumb and finger together and slid them across her lips as if she were closing a zipper. It was their "I won't tell" signal.

Dwayne tugged his hat lower, and Melody crossed the street. When she looked, Dwayne's part of the line had passed the windows, and he was gone.

Melody kept walking and singing. She sang as loud as she could, becoming part of the rhythm of voices. Melody realized that because of her own experience at Fieldston's, she was connected to people she would never know: the people from the past who had been treated unfairly, just as she and Dwayne had been, and people in the future. After all, if their boycott was a success, Fieldston's would change.

Melody was part of that change. She could see her father, lifting his sign into the air as he marched, chanting the same words that she chanted. She thought of the poem Mr. Langston Hughes had read at the book signing and about how her father had given her a love of poetry. Now she knew that both her parents had also given her a love for justice and equality and dignity.

And so, to the rhythm of the words in the air, Melody marched.

The next day at church, Melody's legs were tired from walking, and her arms were tired from holding up her protest sign. But her heart felt stronger because she had been part of something she believed in.

After the service, everyone seemed to be talking about the boycott. "It made the news on the radio," Val said to Melody. "What was it like?"

"There were so many more people there than I expected," Melody explained. "It felt good to be a part of it."

"I wish I'd been there," Val said.

"Me, too," Melody agreed. "Maybe you can come next week."

"I'll ask my parents. I think they'll let me."

Melody smiled. "Did you see any houses you liked?"

Val's face brightened. "I did. There was one with a pink bedroom! But it didn't have a fireplace. Mama and Daddy said we're going to keep looking."

Melody nodded as her cousin talked, but she was giving Val only half her attention. Some of her other friends were heading down to Sunday school. This was her chance to find out what they all thought about her answer to the Challenge to Change.

"Hi, everybody," she said, stopping them at the classroom door. "I have an idea, but I need help."

Sharon leaned in. "What kind of help?"

"What's the idea?" Diane asked.

"The last time you had an idea," Julius said, "you ended up talking in front of the whole Block Club."

Melody took a deep breath and let the words tumble out. "The playground in our neighborhood is a mess, and I want to make it nice again!"

"I didn't know there was a playground," Val said.

Julius nodded. "My dad taught me how to play handball there."

"Nobody goes there anymore," Sharon said. "Maybe we're just too old for jungle gyms!"

"Well, my little sisters aren't," Diane said. "I took

them there last summer, and most of the swings were gone. The one that's left is broken. My mom says it's dangerous."

"When we get our own house, my daddy says we can have a swing set in the backyard," Val said kindly. "You and your sisters can all come over to play."

What Val said made Melody realize something. Most people in their neighborhood had small back-yards. A few had swing sets, but many had vegetable gardens instead, like her family did. She'd heard Poppa say that there just wasn't room for both.

"I think having a fun, safe playground is really important," Melody said. Everyone nodded in agreement.

"If we work together as a team, maybe we could fix it up ourselves," she continued. "We could clean it up, paint the benches, pull out the weeds, and plant flowers—"

"Get new swings," Diane added.

"And maybe do something about the handball courts," Julius said hopefully.

Melody was encouraged. Her friends were getting excited. So she told them the rest of her idea. "What if we start our own club, a kids' block club?"

There was silence for a moment. Then Julius nodded. "Count me in."

"Great idea!" Sharon said.

Diane smiled and nodded her agreement.

"I'll join for now," Val said, "but don't you think we might have to ask permission, or something—President Melody?"

"P-Pres—" Melody stuttered and blinked. *President?* She'd never intended to be a leader, just part of the club. It would be like the choir here at church, where she was one voice among many. Being the president of something meant being a leader—like Miss Dorothy or Pastor Daniels. Melody wasn't so sure she could do that.

"Don't try to get out of it now," Julius laughed. "It was your idea."

"I—um—okay." Melody stammered. "Let's start by asking the grown-ups' Block Club."

Sunday school began, but Melody's mind was still on the playground. Her friends were excited, but they wanted her to lead. Was she ready for that? Melody thought of Yvonne. If only she were here to help.

Help. Hadn't Yvonne told Melody to ask for help from a grown-up? Suddenly, Melody knew just the right person.

Wish List

That afternoon, when Melody took Bo for a walk, they went to Miss Esther's house. After she rang the bell, Melody turned around to look at Miss Esther's view of the park. It wasn't pretty.

When Miss Esther opened the door, she was happy to see Melody. "What a nice surprise!" she said. "Come in, come in."

"Is it okay for Bo to come in, too?" Melody asked. Miss Esther smiled down at Bo, who wagged his tail politely but did not bark.

"I think Bojangles is a well-behaved dog," she said.

"How did you know—"

"It *is* Bojangles, isn't it?" Miss Esther led them into a comfortable-looking living room. "He's named after the dancer, Bill 'Bojangles' Robinson, isn't he?"

Melody nodded her head in wonder. "Yes! We put him on our black history banner. He tap-danced in the movies with Shirley Temple. Mommy says it was a big deal."

Miss Esther nodded. "It was, because he was a black man and she was a little white girl. Movie audiences had never seen that on the screen before. It was an historic moment."

"You know so much about so many things," Melody said. "That's why I came to talk to you."

"What's on your mind, Melody?" Miss Esther sat in a soft armchair near the front window. She gestured toward another chair, and Melody sat, too.

"Do you always sit at this window?" Melody asked.

"I like to see what's going on in the neighborhood."

"Do you like what you see? Over at the park, I mean."

Bo was sitting on the floor beside Melody's chair, looking from her to Miss Esther as if he were following the conversation.

Miss Esther sighed. "I can't say that I do like it, Melody. It's in such bad shape." She leaned forward. "Why do you ask?"

"Well, I sort of have a plan for it."

"I'm so glad to hear it!" Miss Esther said.

Melody scooted to the edge of her chair. "I want to answer the New Year's Challenge to Change by cleaning up the playground and planting a garden. I talked to some of my friends, and they want to help, too. We want to start a Junior Block Club."

"That's a lot of work," Miss Esther said. "Some people might say it's too much for a group of young people like you."

"But it's not!" Melody insisted.

"If you take your idea to the Block Club, you'll need a plan in writing to explain what you hope to do."

"Oh," Melody said, sitting back in her chair. "I don't know how to do that." Suddenly she felt discouraged.

"Well," Miss Esther said, getting up from her chair, "perhaps I can help. Let's start by making a list of everything you'd like to do. I call that the 'wish list,' because sometimes the plan changes and you don't get to do everything you wish you could do."

And with that, Melody and Miss Esther began to work together.

♫

Two weeks later, on the first Friday in March, Melody and her parents walked to Julius's house after dinner for the monthly Block Club meeting. Everyone gathered in the finished basement, where the grown-ups sat on folding chairs around card tables and drank coffee out of paper cups. Melody, Val, Sharon, Diane, and Julius perched on an assortment of stools.

At seven o'clock, Mr. Sterling quieted the group and began the meeting.

"Welcome, folks! I want to start with a quick update about the progress of the Fieldston's boycott. Our actions have shown that we believe every store in our community should respect the people of the community. We had some newspaper reporters asking questions about the boycott last week, and I got a call from one of the TV stations. But we have to keep up the pressure and keep up our protests. We all know that change doesn't happen overnight."

There was applause from the kids and the grown-ups. When the group was quiet again, Mr. Sterling said, "Now, some of the children want to speak."

Melody took a piece of paper out of her pocket. It was the wish list Miss Esther had helped her write.

"Hello," she said, looking around the room. Her father raised his chin and smiled. She saw Miss Esther on the far side of the large room.

"We—all of us up here—would like to ask permission to start a Junior Block Club. The reason, um, our purpose, is to fix up the playground and change that part of our community for everyone."

"What a good idea," Sharon's father said from his seat. "It's a disgrace how the city has let that playground deteriorate." Other parents murmured in agreement.

Diane's mother raised her hand. Melody felt funny giving a grown-up permission to speak. "Yes?" Melody said in her best leader voice.

"Block clubs are not a game," Mrs. Harris said.

"I believe our youngsters have shown great responsibility by their participation in the boycott," Miss Esther said. Her voice was kind but firm.

"Yes, you're right," Mrs. Harris quickly agreed. "I just wonder if the children have a plan."

"Yes, ma'am, we do," Melody said. As she read her wish list aloud, there were nods of approval.

"And we plan to keep an eye on it after we finish,

so it doesn't end up like it is again," Diane added.

Miss Esther tapped her cane on the linoleum floor. "I move that we allow the formation of a Junior Block Club."

Melody's father raised his hand. "I second that motion."

"Good! Let's vote!" Mr. Sterling said. "Raise hands to vote yes to a Junior Block Club."

Melody was holding her breath. Every hand went up.

"The ayes have it! Congratulations, Junior Block Club," Mr. Sterling announced.

Melody turned to her friends. They all jumped off their stools and cheered. Julius started shaking all the girls' hands.

Mr. Sterling cleared his throat. "Now, you *do* need an adult adviser."

"I have already been asked, and accepted that position," Miss Esther said, with another tap of her cane.

"And Melody is our president!" Julius shouted. The adults laughed and clapped again.

Melody's father spoke up. "Well, Junior Block Club, do you think you can have this playground cleaned up and ready for our annual Block Club picnic?"

"The picnic is August first, right?" Julius asked.

"Yes," his father said.

"That's almost five months away," Sharon said, counting on her fingers. "That's a lot of time."

Melody didn't say anything. She knew that growing a garden could take a long time. But her friends were so excited, and they were all eager to help, so Melody nodded her head. "We'll make it work," she said.

Grandfathers and "Grandflowers"

melody and Val were in Big Momma's kitchen helping get Sunday dinner ready. On the ride from church, the girls had told Melody's grandparents all about the Junior Block Club and their plans for the park. Poppa and Big Momma were excited about the way Melody and Val and their friends were answering the Challenge to Change, and they had offered to help.

"Oh, good," Melody had said as the car pulled into the driveway. "Because we don't know how to do some of the stuff we want to."

Now Big Momma's kitchen smelled of baked chicken and homemade rolls. She put the girls to work opening jars of tomatoes and green beans that she and Melody's mother had canned last summer.

"Did you grow all this?" Val asked Melody, pouring

the green beans into a pan for Big Momma to heat.

"I sure did!" Melody said, plucking a tomato up with a fork. "Taste!"

Big Momma pretended not to see as Val gobbled down the tomato and smacked her lips. "Mmmm!" Val said.

The rest of the family trickled in as Melody set the table. When Dwayne arrived, Melody wanted to talk to him about the Fieldston's protest. But before she could say anything, he said, "What's this I hear about Melody becoming president of the Junior Block Club?"

"How did you find out?" Melody asked, setting the penguin-shaped salt and pepper shakers in the center of the table.

"I have my neighborhood connections," Dwayne said, winking. "So tell me, Dee-Dee, what are your plans?"

Melody winked back. "You wait and find out," she said.

After Poppa said grace and they all began to pass the food around, Melody and Val took turns explaining the park project. When they got to the list of things they didn't know how to fix, Melody frowned. "The handball courts are falling apart," she said. "They're made of brick. What should we do?"

"One of my piano students is a bricklayer's son," Big Momma said. "I could talk to him."

"Would you, Big Momma?" Melody asked eagerly. "And Poppa, would you help us decide which plants would grow best in the park?"

"I will," he said, passing the bowl of beans to Charles. "You'll need to draw up a plan of the space so we know how much room we have."

"What about the swings?" Val asked. "We want to get ones that aren't broken."

"I think that replacing the swings is the city's responsibility," Mommy replied. "You can ask the Parks Commissioner. How do you think you can find his name?" she asked in her teacher's voice.

Melody and Val looked at each other and shrugged.

Lila sighed. "The library," she whispered loudly to them. Then Lila looked at Dwayne. "That's a stage whisper, right?" she asked, which made everyone laugh.

Charles took a serving of green beans and looked across the table at Melody's mother. "Frances, this reminds me of all the canning you and Aunt Geneva did when we were kids. The fruit trees!"

"Fruit trees?" Melody asked curiously.

"Oh, yes," her mother said. "Back on the farm we had fig trees, along with plum and peach trees."

"Yes!" Poppa said. "We had quite an orchard."

Big Momma laughed. "And it was quite a lot of work for me every summer, to can all of those fruits and vegetables."

"But they tasted so good," Charles said.

"What else did you grow, Poppa?" Melody asked.

"When I was a young man," Poppa said, "I tried to do it all. We grew a little bit of everything. I had pecan trees and peanuts. Greens of all kinds, beans, tomatoes, potatoes."

"That sounds like a grocery store," Dwayne laughed.

"Yes, it pretty much was," Big Momma said. "In those days, we grew everything we ate. We planted, we weeded, we picked. If we had an extra-large crop of something, we'd share with neighbors."

Melody's mother nodded. "Oh, there was nothing like walking in the shade of the plum trees and plucking off a few to eat right there on the spot!"

"I loved that place," Poppa said, his voice becoming thicker and quieter. "I planted a big flower garden and built a wooden fence arond it." Poppa looked down at his knife and fork for a few minutes, and then looked up again. Everyone had stopped eating to listen.

"See, I'd grown up on that farm. My daddy worked it for a white man. Daddy scrimped and he saved, and he scrimped and he saved. He worked hard. We worked hard with him. I knew how much he wanted to own that place, so I worked extra jobs to help. Together, we finally saved enough to be able to buy a little piece of that land." He looked toward Big Momma, who smiled and put her hand over his on the table.

"Back then it was almost impossible for a Negro to own property," she said. "Not long after they bought the land, Frank's father died. So Frank took over the farm. We had only just gotten married. His sister Beck and his brother Roy—that's Charles's daddy—had already left and moved to Birmingham. I was teaching music at a school during the week and giving piano lessons on the weekends. Your grandfather worked hard day and night to keep the farm going."

"That land was special to me," Poppa said. "It was more than just dirt and trees and plants. It was . . . my life. It had been my daddy's life, and my mama's life. Hardest thing I ever did was leave it. But—"

He looked around at Val and Melody and Lila and Dwayne. "I did it for all of you. I passed it on to all of you."

Lila shook her head. "How could you pass it on, Poppa? We've never even seen it."

"You have it in you," Poppa said to Lila. "It's the way your parents teach you and how you work hard." He turned to Dwayne. "It's what we share, like our love of poetry and music." Finally, Poppa looked at Melody. "It's me, teaching you about plants. How to make them grow tall and strong. How to make things beautiful. And you know what? One day you'll pass my farm on to the children you have."

Poppa tapped his chest. "It's here."

Everyone at the table was quiet. Melody saw Tish dabbing at her eyes with her paper napkin. Big Momma still had her hand over Poppa's. Mommy looked as if she was remembering something from long ago.

"You know what, Poppa?" Dwayne said. "I know

what you mean. It was hard for me to leave home, too."

Lila kicked Melody under the table. For once, Dwayne was very serious.

"I miss all of this, sitting around talking and eating Mom's and Big Momma's great food together, hearing Dee-Dee ask a million questions, and Lila trying to answer all of them. I miss it a lot." He looked at his father. "I even miss you yelling at me about college."

Daddy started to say something, but Dwayne went on.

"But like Poppa said, all of you are here." He tapped his chest. "Right along with my music. So every time I write a song, or sing a song, I've got all the Ellisons and Porters right with me. Dad, I know you think I got into this business for all the wrong reasons, for flash and fame. You were kind of right. It's hard work. I know that you and your father, and Poppa and his daddy—y'all broke your backs working hard to give us something better. An easier life than you had. It's not easy being black, no matter what we choose to do, right? I still believe that music can change things, and I'm not afraid to work hard at something I want. I learned that from you, Dad."

♪ Grandfathers and "Grandflowers" ♪

Melody's father had the strangest expression she'd ever seen on his face. He looked confused and proud all at once. He stared at Dwayne, but neither one of them said a word. Melody didn't quite understand why her mother was smiling.

Melody finally broke the silence. "I'd like to see the farm," she said.

Her grandfather smiled. "And you will, Little One. I'll make sure of it." He turned toward Melody's mother.

"Let's drive down once school is out, Frances. I'll get someone to take care of the shop for a week, and we can stay with my sister."

"I'd love that, Daddy. We could go for Aunt Beck's Fourth of July picnic."

Melody was excited about the trip, but she couldn't help thinking of the playground project. She would be planting flowers in June. Melody was the president, so it was her job to make sure everything got done properly. She put her fork down. *Would a good leader choose not to go to see the farm?* she wondered.

"What's the date today?" Melody blurted out.

Lila rolled her eyes, but Val said, "March eighth."

The Block Club picnic was August first. Even if she was gone for a week, there would be enough time, when she got back, to get everything done.

Melody relaxed. The farm meant a lot to her family, and she wasn't going to miss her chance to see it.

After dessert, Melody went to sit beside her grandfather, on the arm of his big leather recliner.

"Poppa, did you bring any of your seeds up here when you left Alabama?"

"Why, yes, and bulbs too. Those orange daylilies that you like come from roots I brought. You know I call those great-great-grand—"

"—flowers," Melody finished, giggling. "Miss Esther gave me some heirloom seeds that came from her mother's garden," she explained. "Hollyhocks. I think I'd like to plant some along the playground fence, so she can see them from her window. They might remind her of where she came from."

Poppa gave Melody a kiss on top of her head. "I like the sound of that. On Friday, let's skip your work day at the flower shop and go take a look at that playground."

♪ Grandfathers and "Grandflowers" ♪

"That would be great!" Melody cried. "I'll ask Miss Esther and the Junior Block Club to meet us there."

As soon as school was out on Friday, Melody, Val, Diane, Sharon, and Julius raced to the park. While they waited for Melody's grandfather, Melody gave each person a copy of the playground wish list. She had spent all week writing out copies of the one she had made with Miss Esther, and now her friends were studying the pages.

Julius looked up from his copy. "Vegetables?" he asked. "Who plants vegetables in a playground?"

"Melody does," Val said loyally.

Diane shook her head. "I haven't even heard of some of the flowers on this list," she said.

"Me either," Sharon shrugged. "But Melody's the expert."

"No, my grandfather's the expert," Melody said. "And Miss Esther. She suggested some of these plants."

Julius grinned. "As long as the playground stuff gets fixed, I don't care what we grow."

"Here comes Miss Esther now," Sharon said.

The group turned to see Miss Esther crossing the street, her cane in one hand and a shoebox in the other.

Melody rushed to the curb. "Can I help you?" she asked, taking Miss Esther's elbow.

"Thank you, dear," Miss Esther said. "You may take this box. I thought you all might like a little snack after school."

Melody removed the lid. The box was lined with wax paper and filled with slices of banana bread. "Thank you!" she said, smiling.

When Poppa's truck rumbled to a stop in front of the park, the members of the Junior Block Club were all nibbling their second slices of bread. "Hello there," Poppa called. "I see you've started on the important business at hand."

Melody grinned and wiped the crumbs from her hands. "Hi, Poppa." She gave him a copy of the playground wish list.

"Let's do it, then," Julius said, pushing open the creaking, squeaking gate and waving everyone into the park.

They all took a slow walk along the paths, talking

about what needed to be done and checking the list to make sure everything was on it. Poppa and Miss Esther followed, asking questions.

They stopped at a jungle-like area near the jungle gym. "This is where we can plant flowers," Melody said, pointing to a stretch of snow-covered grass next to a tangle of overgrown bushes. "Something really colorful, so that when you're hanging upside down on the jungle gym, it looks like a rainbow!"

"My sisters will love that," Diane said.

"And more flowers there, and there . . ." Melody pointed with her pencil. She looked up at the sky and then spun around. "And since there's full sun over there, we could do vegetables. Right, Miss Esther?"

"You are right, Melody. Now you can draw all this up in your plan."

"Yes, ma'am," Melody said.

"Drawing?" Sharon asked.

Melody had an idea. "Sharon, you are a great artist. Would you draw a plan for our playground?"

Sharon smiled. "Of course I will."

They all moved on to the peeling benches. "You'll need special paint for outdoors," Miss Esther said.

"What about these swings?" Poppa asked.

"I need to write to the Parks Commissioner about that," Melody said.

Poppa folded his arms. "Good. And do you have a budget?"

"Budget?" Julius asked.

"You mean, money?" Diane said, looking at Melody.

Melody's stomach dropped. *Of course we'll need money,* she thought. She'd planned out everything except that.

"I suspect that our Block Club can provide some funds from our budget," Miss Esther said. "I'll bring it up at the next meeting."

Melody was relieved. "Thank you, Miss Esther."

Poppa nodded. "Some local businesses may be willing to donate supplies, too," he added.

Melody brightened. "I can dig up some plants from my garden this spring," she said. "That will save us some money."

"Now you're thinking," Sharon said.

The next morning, Melody and Lila went to the

public library. "Are you going to write that letter to the Parks Commissioner today?" Lila asked as they walked. She struggled with her armload of library books, so Melody reached over to take three off the top.

"Yes, I am. Everybody says getting new swings is up to the city. If the Junior Block Club is going to work hard to clean up the playground, then it's only fair that we get some help. Kids are citizens, too!"

"That's exactly what you should say in your letter," Lila told her.

"Really?" Melody asked. "Lila, would you look my letter over when I'm done?"

"Of course," Lila smiled. "Call it my contribution to the Junior Block Club."

Singing Together

*A*pril came, and it was warm enough for the Junior Block Club to start the cleanup. Poppa had given Melody some old gardening gloves from his workroom, and she had been saving paper grocery bags for trash, dead plants, and twigs. The club members had recruited some other neighborhood kids to help, and Melody had told everyone to wear long pants and long sleeves to the work day.

At nine o'clock on the second Saturday of the month, Melody and Val were the first to arrive at the park. Soon, Sharon came running up the block. A few minutes later, Mrs. Harris pulled up and Diane got out of the car.

"Where's everybody else?" Diane asked.

"I don't know," Sharon said.

Melody was concerned. She pulled out her notebook. "Well, I have the names of nine people who agreed to come. I wonder where Julius is."

"Here I am!" He walked across the street carrying two rakes. "I'm ready! I borrowed these from my dad."

"Good idea," Melody said, realizing that she hadn't thought of bringing rakes. "So, where's everybody else?"

Julius looked around. "Larry and Clifton haven't shown up yet? They promised they'd come."

"Well, I guess we just have to get started," Melody said.

They went through the gate. The park looked pretty much the same as it had the last time they were there, except that the snow was gone. Melody put her box of supplies down on one of the benches. She realized that if everyone had shown up, she wouldn't have had enough gloves.

"Okay." Melody stood with her hands on her hips. "I say we each take a part of the park to work in. Let's call them zones. Julius, you take the handball zone. Sharon, how about you and Val in the swing zone? Diane, do you want to clear the flower beds with me?"

"Nah, I'm not much of a gardener," Diane said. "Sharon, switch with me?"

Sharon shook her head. "No, thanks."

Melody looked at Diane. *Oh, dear,* she thought. *Is there a problem? Already?*

"I'll switch," Val said. "Melody and I have worked in the garden together."

"Deal." Diane nodded.

Thank goodness, Melody thought. Everyone went to their zones, and Melody used one of Julius's rakes to show Val how to carefully clear the layers of dead leaves without damaging anything growing underneath.

As Val got started, Melody took out her transistor radio and turned it on. "Everything goes faster with music," she said, pulling the antenna all the way up. But after a few minutes, the only station that came in clearly was a talk show that no one wanted to listen to.

"We could sing ourselves," Diane suggested. "Then you wouldn't have to run down the battery on your radio."

"Good idea," Melody said, turning back to what had once been a flower bed near the first set of benches.

"What are we going to sing?" Julius yelled.

"A work song," Sharon yelled back.

"Which one?" Melody asked without looking up. Val had uncovered a few tiny green shoots of something poking up among the weeds.

"I know," Diane said. *"If I had a hammer, I'd hammer in the morning . . ."*

Val burst out laughing. "We're not doing construction work!"

"Not yet," Julius said, picking up the song. *"I'd hammer in the evening, all over this **park**!"*

He'd changed the last word, and the rest of the kids giggled. Then they all joined in.

> *I'd hammer out danger,*
> *I'd hammer out a warning,*
> *I'd hammer out love between my brothers*
>   *and my sisters,*
> *All over this land!*

As the verse ended, Melody heard the gate creak and looked up. Miss Esther came in, wearing a gardening apron over her sweater and carrying a pair of pruning shears. Melody was relieved to see her.

"Hello, Junior Block Club," Miss Esther called out.

"Hello, Miss Esther!" the children all called back. It sounded as if they were still singing together.

Miss Esther laughed. "I came to see if you need help identifying which shrubs need pruning," she said.

Melody stood up and looked around. She knew a lot about flowers, but nothing about bushes or shrubs. "Yes, we do," she said.

While Val, Sharon, and Diane kept working, Julius joined Melody. Miss Esther showed them how to hold the shears and where to cut branches so that the plant wouldn't be damaged.

"This is cool stuff," Julius said. "I feel like I'm a farmer."

"I think you would be an *arborist*," Miss Esther told him. "That's someone who takes care of trees. And that is *cool*, as you say."

Julius looked pleased, and Melody smiled.

After an hour, Miss Esther had to leave to go to a church meeting. By that time, Sharon and Diane had quit working and had started climbing on the jungle gym. Everyone was hot from working—and playing—so the group took a break. Everyone was thirsty, too, but no one had brought anything to drink.

"Are we done for the day?" Diane asked, plopping down on one of the worn benches.

"I'm hungry," Julius said. "Maybe I'll head home."

"I have to go, too," Sharon said. "My mom's taking me to buy new shoes. Sorry, Melody," she called as she took off running.

Melody sat down next to Diane and sighed. She was sweaty and dirty and thirsty, and the Junior Block Club hadn't gotten as much done as she'd hoped they would. That's when Melody saw her grandfather's truck.

"Well, there," Poppa said, strolling through the gate carrying a large paper bag. "You all look a bit wilted." He set the bag down on the bench and pulled out a thermos and a stack of paper cups. "How about some water?"

"Thanks, Mr. Porter," Diane and Julius said.

Val joined them, and they all drank the water Poppa poured. Melody hoped Diane and Julius would stay, but after a few minutes, they both left.

Val went back to raking. Melody set her cup down and began to clap the dirt off her gloves. "Boy, this didn't go the way I thought," she mumbled.

"How did you think things would go?" Poppa asked, sitting down beside her.

Melody shook her head. "I thought because I knew about gardening that I'd be a better leader. But I didn't check to make sure everyone would show up. I didn't remember to bring tools. I didn't even bring water!"

"You're learning to be a leader, Little One," Poppa told her. "And being a leader doesn't mean you have to do everything yourself. Julius remembered tools. Why don't you make him head of the tool committee?"

"Really?" Melody asked. "I could do that?"

"Yes. And you could ask someone to remind the block club members when there's a work day."

"Diane would love that," Val piped up. "She's good at being bossy."

"I guess," Melody said slowly. "But if other people do things, doesn't that mean I'm not a leader?"

"This is a big project, and you need many hands," Poppa said. "A good leader helps everyone see that they're a special part of the team. Leading takes patience, just like gardening. And you're right. You're a wonderful gardener. You know how to make things take root and grow. As your club works together, it will become stronger."

Melody nodded. "You make it sound like the Junior Block Club might blossom one day, Poppa."

"Won't it?" he asked.

Melody smiled. She sure hoped so.

Talking to Poppa made Melody feel better. She went home and cleaned herself up, and then she sat down in the living room with her father's book of Langston Hughes poems. She was engrossed in the rhythm of the words when the phone rang.

Mommy called from the bathroom upstairs. "Melody, can you answer that, please?"

Melody picked up the phone. "Hello?"

"Hey, Dee-Dee? It's me, Dwayne."

"I know your voice on the phone, Dwayne," Melody said.

"Oh. Whatcha doing?"

"Reading," she said. "Why are you acting weird?"

"Maybe because I have a little job for you."

Melody put her book down, and all thoughts of

poetry flew from her mind. Dwayne could only be talking about one thing.

"You want me to sing with you?" she asked.

"Well, sing *for* me. For us. Sing backup. Look, Mr. Gordy is finally giving The Three Ravens a chance in the studio to cut our own single." Melody heard the excitement in her brother's voice.

"Can Val come? And Sharon? And Lila? Just to watch?"

"Hey, it's not a stage show, all right? I'll find out. Anyway, Mom or Dad needs to bring you, and one of them has to sign something so that you can work in the studio. I'm gonna copy the lyrics and music and bring them home. Can you be at Motown at four o'clock tomorrow?"

"Tomorrow?!" Melody gasped. "First, it's Sunday. Second, I can't learn a new song by tomorrow! You want me to mess it up?"

Dwayne laughed. "You won't mess up. But I can only get into the studio when they tell me I can. Listen, you check with Mom, see if it's okay."

As soon as Dwayne clicked off, Melody ran upstairs shouting, "Mommy! Mommy!"

"Is the house on fire?" her father mumbled, opening their bedroom door. Melody rushed in.

"No, Daddy. Sorry. Dwayne just asked me to sing backup on his record! Can I? I can't do it without your permission. Please, please!"

Melody's mother opened the bathroom door across the hall. "How wonderful! Will, this would be a great opportunity for Melody. She could see the real work behind the flash."

"Don't try to get me on Dwayne's side, Frances," Melody's father answered. "I still believe a black man can have a better life, an easier life, with a college education. Not a record." Then Daddy looked at Melody. His face softened. "But for you? This sounds like a once-in-a-lifetime chance." He tugged Melody's pigtail. "You may go."

"Thank you, Daddy!" Melody cried. She turned to leave and then stopped and looked at her father again. "What do you think my singing name should be? On the record, I mean?"

Melody's father tilted his head to one side. "Let's see . . . How about Melody Ellison?"

"Daddy!"

"That's the name I give you permission to use," he said.

Melody didn't say another word. She didn't want her father to change his mind.

Dwayne was as good as his word. That evening he came home with a copy of handwritten music and lyrics, a tape recorder and a tape, and the other two members of The Three Ravens. If Daddy hadn't gone bowling, Melody knew he would have been there, grilling Dwayne and his bandmates.

"Hey, lil sis," Artie said with a wave. His hair was different, and Melody had never before seen him wearing pants that weren't blue jeans. Phil seemed to be looking for something, and when footsteps sounded on the stairs, he jerked his head up. *He's hoping Lila's home,* Melody thought, grinning in his direction. *But she's not.* Phil grinned back at her and ducked his head.

Mommy came downstairs. "Hello, boys. This is so exciting! What an opportunity!"

"Thanks, Mom," Dwayne said.

"May I see the lyrics?"

"Sure, Mom." Dwayne handed the sheet to his mother. "It's called 'Move On Up.' It's a good song for Melody."

Melody stuck her chin over her mother's shoulder to look, too. It was the song Dwayne had sung to her on her birthday. Melody stepped back, feeling even more excited.

"This is very nice, Dwayne," Mommy finally said. "I like the positive message."

Dwayne ducked his head, and Melody could see that he looked pleased. "I really didn't think of it like that. It just came into my head, and I wrote it." He handed Melody the cassette tape. "Melody, listen to this and follow along in the music. You'll see where I want you to come in."

Dwayne flipped the tape recorder on, and everyone was absolutely still. Melody had to concentrate very hard to focus on the music instead of her heart, which was pounding with excitement.

At four the next afternoon, a carload of girls and one mom spilled out onto the sidewalk of Grand

Boulevard. Motown's Hitsville U.S.A. studio looked like an ordinary house except for the big display window in front. It was full of posters advertising performances by various Motown artists. Dwayne met the group at the door looking very grown up and serious.

"Is Mr. Gordy here?" Mommy asked.

"He lives upstairs, and he'll probably come down later. Right now it's just us. I wanted to give you a tour before Phil and Artie and the studio musicians arrive."

Dwayne led them through a maze of rooms, explaining what went on in each of them. As Dwayne talked about the songwriters and the people who designed the album covers, Melody began to realize that there was more to making a record than just singing.

The group went down a hallway, up a few steps, and then down a few others, and into a large room whose walls were covered with something that looked like a bulletin board. "Here's the studio," Dwayne said proudly.

"What's that on the walls?" Sharon asked.

"Soundproofing," Dwayne answered. "That way, no car sounds or people's voices from outside can mess up the recording. This isn't really a fancy setup," he said. "But the sound that comes out of here is more than fancy."

"He sounds like he knows what he's talking about," Melody said to Lila.

Lila nodded. "He sounds professional," she said.

There were drums and cymbals in one corner, and other instruments resting against the wall. At one end of the room was a huge piano.

"That's a *grand* piano," Mommy whispered.

Melody imagined that Dwayne must have great fun with such a nice piano, after so many years playing Big Momma's upright and the church piano.

"Can you play a little something for us, Dwayne?" Mommy asked.

Dwayne sat on the bench and positioned his hands over the keys. Melody slid onto the seat beside him.

"Seems like a classic piano should be singing classical tunes," he said, and he began to play music that Melody had only heard on the radio at Big Momma's house.

"Hey, that's Chopin," Lila said. "When did you—"

Dwayne laughed. "When did *you*?" he shot back.

"Who's Chopin?" Melody asked, looking from Dwayne to Lila.

"Frédéric Chopin. He was a composer in the 1800s," Lila explained.

At that moment, Dwayne switched to a fast Motown-sounding tune. Melody moved her shoulders to the music as Dwayne sang.

> *Let me tell you about this girl*
> *With a smile I know.*
> *She's as happy as the crowd*
> *At a carnival show.*

Dwayne nudged Melody and grinned. *"That's why she's my very special Melody,"* he sang.

"Are you singing about *me*?" Melody asked. She looked at Sharon and Val, who were clapping along.

"Well, isn't that a surprise?" Mommy said.

Melody gave her brother a hug. "What's my song called?"

"'Special Melody,' of course," Dwayne said. He nodded to Lila. "Don't worry. I'm working on songs for you and Vonnie, too."

Lila smiled, and Melody knew she was impressed.

Val pointed at a small window that looked down on the room. "What's that?" she asked. "Who's up there?"

"That's the control room," he said. "Those are the sound engineers, and they hear everything." Dwayne got up and crossed the room, motioning Melody to follow. "See these X's back here on the floor? This is where you'll stand. This microphone will be yours. Phil and Artie will be over here. I'll be at the piano."

"How come Melody's so far from the piano?" Lila asked suspiciously.

Dwayne smiled. "Those folks who work up in that control room know their business. Trust me, you'll hear Dee-Dee. And us and the instruments, too. It's what they call mixing the sound."

Just then, Artie and Phil came into the studio. Phil stopped and said hello to Lila. Then he turned to Dwayne. "I know we only planned for lil sis to do backup, but how about if the others hang out with us and dance? That will give us a great vibe."

Sharon's and Val's eyes grew wide. Lila smiled.

Dwayne thought for a moment. "Yeah. Okay." He said, nodded. "Let's try it."

A soft-spoken lady appeared from somewhere. "Dwayne, may I take your guests upstairs now? The musicians are just about ready to start."

"Thank you," Dwayne said. "My mom is the only one going up to the booth."

"You girls do what Dwayne says," Mommy instructed. Then she blew Melody a kiss before following the lady out.

Sharon, who had been very quiet the whole time, turned to Melody. "This is amazing. You are gonna be so great!"

"Thanks," Melody said, grinning. She was nervous, but she was excited, too.

Dwayne put his hand on Melody's shoulder and guided her to the X he'd pointed out earlier. "So, we're just gonna do this like we're hanging around in our backyard, got that?"

"Got it," Melody said.

The studio began to fill with the other musicians, who talked and laughed as they picked up their instruments. They didn't pay much attention to Melody or the other girls. Most of them were much older than Dwayne. But when Dwayne sat down at the piano,

Melody could tell that he became the leader. He wasn't bossy or rude. When he spoke, his voice was a man's voice, and the others listened.

"Fellas, I have some family in the studio today. And we've changed this up a little bit from last time since our backup singer is here." He motioned toward Melody.

All the musicians turned to her with interest. Because of what Dwayne had said, the musicians thought of her as a real musician, too—not just a kid. Melody stood a little taller.

A voice filled the studio over a loudspeaker. It was coming from the control room. "Dwayne, Mr. Gordy wants to know if you're going to go right in, or riff a little first," the voice said.

"Riff, Mr. Gordy."

Berry Gordy is in there, Melody thought. *He's listening!*

Dwayne looked at Melody over the piano. "How're you feeling? Good?"

She nodded, and he began a jazzy tune, making it up as he went. Improvising, Big Momma called it. Melody felt herself moving to the rhythm.

"One. Two. One, two, three, four," Dwayne counted, and he was into the song. Melody closed her eyes, and when it was time, she sang. And sang. At the end of the second verse, Melody suddenly didn't hear Artie or Phil behind her, only Dwayne's piano. As he picked up the tempo of the music, Melody blinked her eyes open.

"*Move on up,*" he sang, nodding at her.

"*Move on up,*" Melody repeated, feeling happiness bubble up inside. She knew just what Dwayne was "calling," and it was her job to "respond" by singing whatever he sang in harmony. She'd heard the adult choir at church sing this way, and it always excited the congregation.

"*Yeah, I'm movin'! I'm movin'!*" Dwayne's fingers flew on the keys as he smiled at her.

"*Yeah, I'm movin'! I'm movin'!*" Melody sang back.

Dwayne threw one of his hands into the air while still playing smoothly with the other.

Artie's and Phil's voices came back in, singing, "*It's time to moooovvve.*"

Melody saw Sharon and Val and Lila dancing, and she grinned so wide that her face hurt. Dwayne hit the final notes, and then everything was still. After a moment, all the musicians cheered.

"That was something, Dwayne!"

"Hey, great. What a bunch of raw talent!"

"Man, that is going to be a hit!"

Melody danced toward her brother, still feeling the music. "Was I okay?" she asked.

"Not okay," he said.

Melody stopped dancing, but Dwayne pulled her into a bear hug. "You were perfect, Dee-Dee. And you made our record perfect, too."

Melody spun around. The musicians and Lila and her friends were clapping. She glanced up at the window of the sound booth and saw her mother clapping and waving. The other people in the booth looked pleased.

As she looked around, she wondered how many wonderful, talented singers had stood in this very place, on that same X. Melody didn't think she'd ever be a professional singer, and she would never be famous. But she loved singing, and she knew that she'd helped Dwayne get a little closer to his dream. She was overjoyed at that.

Open Doors

*O*n the following Saturday, Melody arrived at the playground pulling her old red wagon. In it was a thermos of water, some paper cups, a box of graham crackers, and a bag of apples. At the gate, she met Julius and a couple of his friends. They were carrying armloads of gardening tools. She smiled as Julius gave her a thumbs-up sign.

"Hi, Melody!" Diane greeted her just inside the park. "Today we have two third-graders, five fourth-graders, and two sixth-graders, not including Val, Sharon, or Julius. I called everyone yesterday to remind them. And I took attendance today."

"Thanks, Diane," Melody said. "You made sure we have plenty of hands for our work day." Melody rolled the wagon near one of the benches. Her grandfather had been right, again. Once she asked her friends to do the things they were good at, they were even more interested in working on the work days. Now Melody could concentrate on the garden plan.

"Good morning, everybody!" Melody called out.

"'Morning, Melody!" everyone shouted back. But no one stopped working.

Melody walked around the paths, noticing where tiny new plants were breaking through the earth in the spring sun. She pulled out her pad and pencil to make notes, humming Dwayne's new song as she went. Soon, everyone else had picked up the tune and was humming along with her, without even knowing the words.

As Melody passed her, Val whispered, "Good job getting publicity for Dwayne's record!"

Melody grinned. "Wait until they hear the real thing!"

"Dwayne still doesn't know when he's going to have the record," Melody told Val a few days later. "He said Mr. Gordy doesn't release anything that's not perfect. They're still mixing the sound."

Melody was spending the night with Val at Poppa

and Big Momma's because of a school holiday. Melody's grandparents were having their evening coffee in the kitchen, and Val and Melody were putting a jigsaw puzzle together while they watched TV.

"I know, I know. I just want to be the first person to hear it," Val said.

Melody laughed. "You'll probably be about the hundredth, after all the people at Motown listen to it, and then Mommy, and then Daddy, and Big Momma and Poppa and your parents and Yvonne and all her friends . . ."

"You're so silly sometimes," Val said. "Only not when you're talking about the playground. Did you get an answer to your letter yet?" she added.

Melody shook her head. "It seems like it's taking a long time. It's hard to wait."

"I know what you mean," Val said, fitting a piece into the puzzle. "I guess a challenge isn't a challenge if it's easy."

"I guess. We need to keep working anyway. The weather's getting warmer, and Poppa said we'll be able to dig up some daylilies from my yard to transplant into the park. And I was thinking—"

Melody stopped talking because there was a commotion in the kitchen. Val's parents had come in the back door. "This is it, Charles!" Val's mother cried.

"We haven't even seen it, Tish," Val's father replied. "We can't make an offer yet."

"Well, our new real estate agent set up a showing for tomorrow morning."

Val raised her eyebrows and then raised her self. "Let's find out what's going on," she said.

Val's parents were standing by the table. There was an open folder in front of Tish, and Melody saw a page full of numbers.

"We may finally be getting somewhere with this real estate agent who works with the Fair Housing Committee," Tish was saying to Poppa and Big Momma. "The people selling this house are white, but the agent said they're willing to sell to any buyer who has the money regardless of race."

Big Momma nodded. "You should be able to buy any house you can afford anywhere you choose. That's what Dr. King said last year when he was here in Detroit. That's what the law should say, too."

"Mama?" Val asked eagerly. "Is this it? Is this the

house we've been waiting for?"

"I hope so, baby," Tish answered "I've seen pictures, and I think it's perfect." She looked at Val's father. "I think we should offer to buy it."

"And I think we should look at it first," Charles replied.

"We will," Tish answered. "First thing in the morning."

Val's face lit up. "Can Melody and I go?" she asked. "We don't have school tomorrow."

"I don't see why not," Tish replied.

It took Melody and Val a long time to fall asleep that night. They kept whispering about the bubble-gum-pink bedroom Val wanted. "I hope this is it," Val said before finally dozing off.

In the morning, Val was wide awake when Melody opened her eyes. "I can't wait anymore! Let's go!"

The girls got dressed and hurried downstairs. Tish was in the kitchen dressed in a blue suit and high heels, her hair pulled back in a smooth ponytail. Charles was wearing a suit and tie and looked nervous.

♫ Open Doors ♫

Big Momma poured the girls bowls of cereal,
and they sat at the table while the grown-ups drank
their coffee. Val ate quickly, without saying a word.
"Let's go!" she said, standing up the moment she was
finished. Everyone laughed.

Melody and Val and her parents drove quite a
distance through different neighborhoods that Melody
had never seen. She noticed that the farther away
they got from her grandparents' house, the larger the
houses and yards were. There were big shade trees
everywhere.

"There's lots of room for my swing set in these
yards," Val murmured.

"Yes, there is," Melody said. She thought again
about the small yards in her own neighborhood. This
was why the park project was so important. Lots of
kids needed a place to play.

"Look, there it is," Tish said, pointing. "It's two
stories, just like we want, and it has a fireplace."

Charles parked and they got out. The house looked
welcoming. It had a front porch and a big bay window.

"There's our real estate agent," Charles said, nodding at the white woman by the front door.

Melody didn't find the empty rooms very interesting, but when they got to the backyard, she got excited. It was huge. There were two shade trees at the back, but there was plenty of room for flowers and vegetables, and lots of sunshine.

"What do you think?" Charles stood behind the girls at the back door.

"Swing set!" Val shouted.

"Garden!" Melody said.

Charles called over his shoulder to Tish and the real estate agent. "It's time to buy ourselves a house!"

Val's parents took the girls to Melody's house and then went to the agent's office to "write an offer." Neither Melody nor Val knew what that meant, but they were both glad they didn't have to go along.

The girls went to the kitchen for a snack, and there on the table was a long white envelope addressed to Melody. It had a seal with the words "City of Detroit" in the corner.

"I bet it's an answer from the Parks Commissioner!" Val said. "Finally! Open it!"

♪ Open Doors ♪

"We're going to get our swings!" Melody said with excitement. She read the letter to Val.

> *April 17, 1964*
> *Dear Miss Ellison,*
>   *We regret to inform you that due to*
> *budget constraints, the Parks Department*
> *will not be able to replace the swings in your*
> *neighborhood park. Thank you for being*
> *a concerned citizen.*

Melody stopped reading. She couldn't believe it. "They said no."

"What's a constraint?" Val asked.

"I'm not sure," Melody said. "But it can't be good." She was angry. "They thank me for being a concerned citizen, but they won't help? That's not fair."

Val shook her head. "What are we going to do now?"

"Meet with the Junior Block Club," Melody said. "Right away."

Melody called an emergency meeting that afternoon, and everyone gathered at Miss Esther's house. Melody read the letter out loud.

"This is so unfair," Sharon said.

Diane nodded. "It's wrong. Do you think the Parks Department said no because the park is in a black neighborhood?"

The kids looked at one another. "That doesn't make any sense," Melody said. She turned to Miss Esther, who hadn't said anything yet. "Is that why?"

"That's an important question," Miss Esther said thoughtfully. "Sometimes Negro neighborhoods don't get the same services as other neighborhoods. Trash isn't picked up as often, and potholes don't get repaired as quickly. One of the reasons we have a Block Club is to ask these sorts of questions. We have to call attention to things that aren't right and then figure out how to fix them."

The group was quiet, and Melody could see that everyone was as disappointed as she was.

"So how do we fix this?" Julius finally asked. "This is our big Challenge project and we can't even do it."

"That's not entirely true," Miss Esther said gently.

"You can't do everything you want all at once, but you have already accomplished quite a bit."

Melody remembered something Miss Esther had said earlier. "Miss Esther's right," Melody told the Junior Block Club. "New swings were on our wish list, but we didn't get them. That doesn't mean we give up. It means we change our plan."

"Okay," said Julius. "What's the new plan?"

"There's still a bunch of stuff to clean up," Diane said.

"We haven't painted the benches yet," Val added.

"And we have a lot of planting to do," Melody said.

Miss Esther nodded. "Even if the swings can't be used, the structure doesn't have to be an eyesore," she said. "You could plant around it."

Melody liked that idea. "Yes—we could plant something that would climb up, like morning glories! Let's keep working," Melody said. "How many can meet after school tomorrow?"

Everyone raised their hands, including Miss Esther.

"Good," Melody said, feeling hopeful again.

After school the next day, Melody and her friends hurried home to change their clothes. On her way to the park, Melody stopped at her grandparents' house to get Val, and the two of them headed to the playground.

When they turned the corner, Melody saw everyone from yesterday's meeting standing outside the gate. *What are they waiting for?* she wondered.

When Sharon started to run toward her, Melody knew that something was wrong.

"What is it?" Melody said when Sharon got to her side.

"Come and see." Sharon pulled her to the park entrance. The gate was closed, and on it was a big fat padlock.

Melody gasped. "What happened?" she asked.

"Read that," Julius said angrily, pointing to a sign posted on the gate.

"Closed by the Parks Department," Melody read. "What does that mean? Closed for today? For the weekend?"

"I don't know," Julius said, "but it stinks."

Miss Esther was making her way across the street. "Hello, children," she called wearily. "I saw a truck from the city pull up this morning. The inspector walked all around the park, and he looked at the broken swing. I believe he thought it was dangerous. That's when he put a lock on the gate."

"But why would he close the whole park?" Melody asked. "The swing's been like that forever! Didn't he see all the work we've done?"

Diane nodded. "They could have just taken that swing away, and let us keep everything else."

Melody was disappointed, but she was also angry. There was no other playground close enough to walk to in their neighborhood.

"Now what?" Julius asked.

Melody had no idea.

More Letters

elody could hardly pay attention in school the next day. All she could think about was the lock on the gate. Miss Esther had suggested that the Junior Block Club write several letters to the Parks Commissioner. "The more letters he gets, the more likely he is to listen," Miss Esther had told them. Everyone had agreed to write, but Melody hadn't started her letter yet. It didn't seem as though the city was going to help a bunch of kids, after all.

When Melody got home, she'd gotten a letter of her own, from Yvonne. Melody took it up to her room, flipped on her radio, and listened to The Supremes while she read.

April 18, 1964
Dear Melody,

*I had my interview for the Summer
Project in Mississippi. It went well, and I
really hope I get accepted. Now that I know
more about the program, I've decided I want
to volunteer with the Freedom Schools. It
will be a lot of work—especially since I've
never taught before. (Unless you count the
fact that I taught Lila everything she knows
about hair. Ha ha.)*

*But you know what? You've inspired me.
You took on the playground project even
though you've never done anything like
it before. You're my role model, Dee-Dee.
Pretty soon everybody's going to be talking
about the park and all the work you and your
friends have done.*

*Keep me posted on all your progress,
Love, Vonnie*

Melody couldn't believe it. Yvonne thought *she* was
a role model? Her brave, smart, strong big sister was
inspired by what Melody was doing? For a moment,
Melody was flattered. Then she sighed. Yvonne didn't

know that the Junior Block Club was locked out of the park. What would Yvonne say if she knew about that "progress"?

The song on the radio ended, and a woman's voice filled Melody's room. "This is Martha Jean the Queen." Melody loved her smooth voice. Martha Jean Steinberg was one of the most popular DJs in Detroit. Any song she played became a hit, and anything she discussed on her show was what grown-ups all over the city talked about. Melody imagined the Queen one day introducing Dwayne's music. Everyone in Detroit would be singing his song.

Wait a minute, Melody thought. She reread Yvonne's letter. *"Pretty soon everybody's going to be talking about the park and all the work you and your friends have done."* If more people knew that the city had closed the park, maybe they would write to the commissioner, too.

Melody needed help letting others know about the problem. She got a clean piece of paper and a pencil. "Dear Miss Steinberg," she began.

A week passed, and the lock was still on the park

gate. Melody was worried that every day they spent not working on the playground meant they were getting further and further away from having the park done in time for the picnic. They hadn't done any planting yet, and Melody was afraid that the garden wouldn't be ready.

Melody dragged around the house after school one day, feeling very out of sorts. She finally decided to go to the backyard to start turning over the soil in her own flower beds. Working in the dirt always helped her feel calm and peaceful. She'd just put on her gloves and taken out her small rake when her mother drove up.

"Is the park still locked?" Mommy asked, her keys jangling as she took her school things out of the car.

Melody nodded her head. "Is this my fault?" she asked her mother. "I'm the one who told the Parks Department about the broken swing."

"The lock on the park gate is not your fault," Mommy said, setting her books on the back step and sitting down. "Even a good leader can't make every-thing go right. You had a wonderful idea; you got people to trust you and work with you. No way is that a failure, and no way is what happened your fault."

"Thanks, Mommy," Melody said. "I just miss working in the park."

"Well, since you've got some time on your hands, you can help Val move into her new room."

Melody's eyes were wide. "Her what? Did they finally buy a house?" she shouted.

Mommy nodded. "I stopped at your grandparents' on my way home, and Charles and Tish just found out. It's official. They bought a house!"

Melody had never experienced a moving day before, and on a bright Saturday in May, when she stood looking out of the picture window of Val's new living room, she felt as if she was at a circus.

"Look!" Val cried, waving wildly at the man who was getting out of the moving van. The huge truck that had pulled up in front of the neatly mowed yard was the biggest Melody had ever seen. She counted eighteen wheels.

"Mama! They're here. They're here!" Val shouted. Melody knew that her cousin was excited to see her things again. Most of her family's belongings had been in storage in Alabama for more than a year.

Tish, Big Momma, and Mommy had been busy cleaning and hanging curtains, but now they all trooped out to the front porch. Charles and Daddy were by Charles's car, unloading boxes of the belongings the family had had at Big Momma's.

"You girls stay right there, out of the way," Charles told them. He went over to the moving truck. The girls watched the moving men open the back door, put up a ramp, and then begin to unload. Off came boxes and beds and chairs.

"Where's *my* stuff?" Val said anxiously.

"All the boxes look the same," Melody said. And then a bicycle was rolled out.

"Oh!" Val ran down the steps, with Melody right behind. Before the grown-ups could say anything, Val had grabbed her bike and wobbled up the driveway toward the backyard. "The tire's flat!" she called, but Melody could tell that Val was still excited.

Melody stood aside to let the men carry a blue-and-gold-striped sofa in, followed by a blue-and-white kitchen table. Next came a pink chair with a fluffy cushion. Melody smiled to see furniture in both Val's and Tish's favorite colors. Melody watched the men come back out and then carry a series of boxes in, heading up the stairs. These boxes were all labeled "Valerie's Room."

The movers carried a twin bedframe and mattress upstairs, and Val's and Melody's fathers followed. A few minutes later, they came back outside. "Princess," Charles said. "You and Melody can start unpacking now!"

Val and Melody practically flew into the house and up the steps. In the bedroom, Val's bed had been put together, but the mattress was bare. The fluffy pink chair was in the middle of the floor, and an empty bookcase and a chest of drawers stood against one wall.

Melody didn't think cleaning her own room was fun. But unpacking Val's boxes was like unwrapping birthday gifts. By the time Tish called them to lunch, Val's clothes were put away, her books were on the shelves, and she and Melody had made the bed and arranged a row of stuffed animals across it.

"It's our first meal in our new home," Tish said as the girls arrived downstairs. As they sat down in the dining room, the doorbell rang.

"Our first guest!" Tish said, hurrying to answer.

"What does that make us?" Daddy asked.

Charles laughed. "You're the family help!" he said. Melody could see that Charles was very happy.

"Congratulations!" Big Momma said. Poppa was behind her, carrying a huge dracaena plant.

"Thank you, Aunt Geneva, Uncle Frank," Charles said.

"Come in," Tish said. "Sit down. Have something to eat." She was beaming.

"I have a present, too!" Melody piped up. She pushed away from the table to find her mother's bag in the living room, and returned with a package that she'd wrapped and tied with pink ribbon.

"Is this a calendar for my new kitchen?" Tish asked as she opened the gift.

"Yes. I marked the week that Val and I are going to Alabama with Poppa and Mommy," Melody said. "And I marked today's date—May 16—too. I think it should be a family holiday." Everyone laughed, and Val took the pink ribbon to tie in her hair.

"Wait!" Melody's father said. "Our housewarming gift is in the kitchen." He left the table with everyone watching curiously. Soon they heard the crackle and static of a radio being turned on and tuned.

"Thank you, Will!" Tish said. "Now, come on back here and eat."

Everyone talked at once, and everyone was talking about the house. Charles told them that one neighbor had actually come by to say hello.

"It may take time to get to know everyone," Tish said. "But we love our new home."

There was a commercial on the radio, and when it was over, Martha Jean the Queen came on the air. "Welcome, Greater Detroit area!" she said.

Tish stopped talking and turned toward the kitchen. "Oh, I love the Queen's program! She plays the best music, and she brings up such interesting topics. We listen to her all the time in the salon."

"Turn up the sound, Charles," Big Momma said.

Martha Jean's voice got louder. "Let's give our support to a group of children from New Hope Baptist Church who banded together to do something special for their community. They asked the Parks Department for new swings. Not only did they get turned down, but they got locked out of their playground! It's a shame that the city and our wonderful mayor can't help these children who have worked *so* hard to improve their neighborhood. Call in if you agree."

Everyone turned to look at Melody and Val.

"That's us!" Val said. "How did she know?"

Melody grinned. "I wrote another letter. But this time I sent it to someone who would talk about our park."

"Melody to the rescue," Melody's mother said.

On the last Thursday in May, Melody received another long white envelope with the city seal in the corner. She tore it open and let out a shriek of joy. Melody called Sharon, Val, Diane, and Julius and asked them to meet her at the park right away.

When Melody got to the park, everyone else was there. "Melody, look!" Julius shouted. "The lock's gone!"

"I know," Melody said. "Listen, everybody."

May 26, 1964
Dear Miss Ellison,

As a result of the many telephone calls and letters we have received about your local park, our inspectors have reviewed the conditions there. After removing the broken swing, we have determined that the park is safe for recreation. Thank you for being a good citizen.

"Let's get back to work!" Melody said, waving the letter in the air. She looked over at the yellow house. Miss Esther stood in the front window, smiling and waving.

After the lock came off the gate, the Junior Block Club sprang into action. That Saturday, a group of dads replaced the missing bricks in the walls of the handball courts with the help of Julius, Diane, and Sharon. While that was happening, Val, Melody, and Miss Esther planted more flowers. Poppa came and helped start the vegetable garden.

Things were looking good. On the next work day, Julius's older brother brought cans of paint and brushes. By then, some moms and kids were coming in to see everything, so Melody made big signs with leftover butcher paper that said: WET PAINT. Then it rained, so they had to do it all over again.

Whenever Melody went to the park to work, she took her transistor radio with her. And it was *always* tuned to Martha Jean the Queen's show.

Important Work

chool ended in the middle of June, and Melody's mother announced to the family that they'd have a "Whatever You Want to Eat" dinner. Lila made bologna and cheese sandwiches with the crusts cut off from the bread. Melody and her mother baked cupcakes, which Melody was allowed to eat *before* she had anything else. Her father picked up hamburgers from his favorite restaurant.

"Well," Mommy said, "we've reached the end of another school year."

"And what a year!" Daddy said, piling French fries onto his plate. "Lila got a science scholarship. Melody took on a playground project. And Yvonne is going to be a teacher this summer."

Yvonne had called home to tell them she'd been accepted to the Mississippi Summer Program. Instead of coming home when her college classes were finished, she'd stayed in Alabama. Now Yvonne was in Ohio for training.

"Everyone kept their grades up, too," Mommy added. "I'm proud of all you girls."

"Well, Lila got straight A's," Melody said. "As usual."

"And you did a lot of work at the park," Lila said, swiping one of Melody's cupcakes.

Melody slapped her sister's hand playfully. "You mean you went to check it out?"

"Of course I did. If the Ellison name is on something, it has to be good!"

Melody made a face. "The Ellison name—"

"—is on the latest Motown record!" Dwayne banged in through the kitchen door waving a small black disc. "Here it is, for your ears only."

"It's out!" Mommy cried.

"Let's hear it right now!" Lila shouted.

Melody jumped up from her chair. "How does it sound?" She raced Dwayne to the record player. He slipped the record out of its paper sleeve, but he held it above Melody's head.

"By the way, Dee-Dee," Dwayne said, "are you having any special entertainment for your playground opening? You know, like live music?"

Melody pretended she didn't know what he was talking about. "Live music? Oh, we don't have a budget for that," she teased. "But if you want to perform for free, we could work something out."

Even Daddy laughed at that.

"Listen to you, Miss President!" Dwayne said.

"I want to listen to *you*," Melody replied, grabbing at Dwayne's record. He handed it to her and let her place it on the turntable. She started the record player, and everyone listened.

> *Girl, it's time that I move,*
> *Time for movin' on up.*
> *Move on up!*
> *Yeah, it's time for my move,*
> *Time to start changing my luck.*
> *Move on up!*

When the song was over, Daddy pushed back his chair, got up, and shook Dwayne's hand. "I'm proud of you, son," he said, his voice full of emotion. "You did what you set out to do. Keep on doing it."

A week before their trip to Alabama, Melody's father was watching television in the living room while Melody and her mother sat at the dining room table talking about what they needed to pack. "That reminds me, Will," Mommy said during a commerical. "Would you bring the suitcases up from the basement?"

"Will do!" Daddy answered, and Melody laughed at his favorite joke. "I'll go down after the news."

The commercial ended and a silver-haired news-caster looked up from his desk. "In national news today, the search continues for three young civil rights workers who are missing in Mississippi."

"What?" Daddy said.

"Mississippi?" Melody repeated. "That's where Yvonne is going," she said in a small voice.

Mommy got up and went into the living room. Melody followed.

"According to CORE, the Congress for Racial Equality, James Chaney, 21, Andrew Goodman, 20, and Michael Schwerner, 24, were investigating the burning of a Negro church in the area. CORE members say the men were arrested on June twenty-first without cause, held in jail for several hours, and then released. The trio has not been seen or heard from since."

Melody felt the same knot in her tummy that she'd felt when she heard about the four little girls who had died in the church bombing in Birmingham.

"Oh, my goodness," Mommy said.

"Do you think they're all right?" Melody asked.

Mommy shook her head. "I don't know, Melody."

Melody tried to make sense of what she'd just heard. It frightened her to think that civil rights workers could just disappear. Then Melody had a horrible thought. "Do you think *Vonnie* is all right?" she asked.

"I pray she is safe," Mommy said. But she looked very concerned.

"There's one way to find out," Daddy said, getting up. "Where's her phone number, Frances?"

"By the phone, on the yellow paper," Mommy answered. She and Melody followed him to the kitchen.

Daddy picked up the phone and dialed. "Hello?" he said. "Yes, this is Will Ellison, Yvonne Ellison's father.

I'd like to speak to her, please."

Melody stood beside her mother, waiting to hear that Yvonne was okay. The seconds seemed to tick by slowly. Daddy tapped impatiently on the telephone receiver. Melody could tell that he was nervous, too.

"Yvonne!" Daddy finally said. He looked at Melody and smiled. Mommy sighed.

"How's everything going?" Daddy asked. He began to nod. "We just heard about that on the news."

Melody turned to her mother. "Do you want Vonnie to come home?" she asked.

Mommy shook her head. "Even if I did, Melody, Yvonne is a strong person, and she makes her own choices now. The work she's decided to do is very important, but the struggle for justice isn't easy. Your sister is becoming a grown-up."

Mommy pulled Melody into a hug. "Mothers and fathers always hope that their children will be safe and make good choices, no matter how old they are. We hope that for all of you."

Melody's tummy settled down. Yvonne was brave and strong and smart, and Melody knew she would make good choices.

Standing Tall

e're going to pass Birmingham and go straight to the farm," Poppa told the girls. "I want to see it before nightfall."

Melody was stiff from sitting in the car for so long. The trip had taken almost twelve hours. They had left Detroit long before sunrise so that they could get to Alabama in the daylight.

Poppa turned off the paved highway and onto a dirt road. They drove for another hour. Melody was surprised when Poppa slowed down next to an empty field, turned onto a rutted path, and stopped the car. Without saying a word, he and Melody's mother got out.

Val looked at Melody, confused. "This looks like nowhere," she said, not moving.

Melody nodded, but she stumbled out to stretch.

Although she'd never been here before, there was something that felt familiar to Melody. Maybe it was the wildflowers dotting the field with shades of yellow and bright blue. They reminded her of the flowers in her own yard as well as the garden at the park. *I hope Sharon and Diane remember to water everything,* Melody thought.

"It's hotter here than it is in Birmingham!" Val said, climbing out of the car and pulling on a sun hat.

"Poppa?" Melody called. "When will we get to your old farm?"

Her grandfather didn't answer. He'd stopped to stare off at something Melody and Val couldn't see.

Melody's mother turned to them. "This is it," she said.

Melody looked around in surprise. There was no orchard. There was no beautiful flower garden surrounded by the wooden fence Poppa had built. In fact, nothing here was the way her grandparents had described. All Melody could see were a few old trees and a dusty path cutting through the grass.

Melody walked over to her grandfather and tugged on his sleeve. "Is it gone?"

Poppa shook his head. "No. It's here," he said, as he tapped his heart. Then he bent to scoop up a handful of dirt. "And here," he said, letting the dirt run through his fingers. "You're standing on it. Standing on the shoulders of all our people who came before."

Melody looked down at her dusty sandals, imagining her grandfather as a boy, and his parents, and maybe even their parents, walking on this same path. She looked up at Poppa, and tried to stand just a little bit taller than she had before.

Melody's mother and grandfather began to walk, and the girls followed in the late afternoon heat. The road curved, and Poppa pointed. Mommy took off her sunglasses and shaded her eyes. In the distance was an old building, and beyond it another field.

"Is that your house?" Melody asked her mother.

"No," her mother said. "Aunt Beck told us that a tree fell on the house during a storm about ten years ago. The house was too damaged to repair, so what was left was torn down."

"That's awful," Melody said, frowning.

"It was," her mother said. "But I still have great memories."

Melody thought of the good times she'd shared with Yvonne and Dwayne and Lila in their home. She knew she wouldn't forget any of that, even if their house was gone.

"So what's that building, then?" Val asked.

"I think it's the old barn," Mommy said.

"That's just what it is," Poppa said in a firm voice. He started walking toward it.

They all followed the rough road. The wildflowers ended, and there was a rickety wood and wire fence on either side of the path.

"Remember coming along here in the wagon, Frances?" Poppa asked.

"You pulled Mommy in a wagon?" Melody asked.

Melody's mother laughed. "Our horse, Sugarfoot, pulled the wagon, sweetie. I sat in back with bushel baskets of peas and sacks of peanuts."

"That was before we got the truck," Poppa explained as he strode along. "Doesn't look like any-one's farmed the land in a long while. I guess the fellow I sold to ended up selling, too. It's a shame." Poppa shook his head. "This was such rich land."

The road ended in a gravel clearing, and the barn

sat in the middle of it. The girls stopped and watched Poppa try the door. It didn't budge. He walked the length of the front, peering into two dusty windows.

"It looks sad," Val whispered. Melody agreed.

"Everything is different," Mommy said. "I can't even tell where the house was." Then Melody's mother did something strange. She walked to a corner of the barn, closed her eyes, and marched into the tall grass.

"Is she *counting*?" Val asked.

Melody watched her mother's mouth move. "Yes, she is!"

"Daddy!" Melody's mother called. "The house was over here!" Poppa and the girls hurried to the edge of the grass where Mommy stood.

"You're right, Frances. Good detective work!"

"So that must be the stump of the tree that fell," her mother said. She pointed away from the barn toward a dark mound overgrown with weeds. "It must have been that old oak, Daddy—the one you hung my swing on!"

Melody had never seen Mommy like this. For the first time, she thought of her mother as Frances Porter, a girl who'd flown in the air on her swing, canned fruits and vegetables, and ridden behind a horse named Sugarfoot.

"This way, girls!" Poppa called, heading past the barn. Despite the heat, he walked quickly.

Melody, Val, and Mommy hurried to follow Poppa. When they rounded the barn, Melody saw a broad grin stretch across Poppa's face, making his silver mustache twitch.

"Well, I'll be!" Melody's mother said. "The pecan trees!"

"There's some farm left, after all," Poppa said.

"Did you plant them all?" Melody asked.

"My father and I did," he said. He smiled at Melody. "Just like you and I plant tomatoes every year."

Melody smiled, too. "Tradition," she whispered.

They all walked a long way through tall grass to reach the trees. Their trunks were fat, gnarled, and gray, but their branches stretched up and spread wide across the sky.

"My pecan trees," Poppa said, touching one of the trunks.

"Melody," her mother said. "You and Val go over and stand with Poppa so I can get a picture."

The grass tickled Melody's legs as she ran toward her grandfather. He put one arm around Melody's shoulders and another around Val's. Just before Mommy snapped the photo, Melody reached out to rub her hand against the pecan tree.

It was nightfall by the time they drove back into Birmingham, to the little green house where Poppa's sister, Aunt Beck, lived. They'd just gotten out of the car when Aunt Beck threw open her screen door. Her long silver braid was wound neatly around her head, and her eyeglasses were perched on her nose.

"I declare, Frank! What took you so long? I've had supper waiting for these babies"—she paused to squeeze Melody and Val in one tight hug—"for hours!" she continued. "Where have you been?"

Melody laughed at the idea of her grandfather having a big sister. When Poppa mumbled his answer, he sounded just like Dwayne talking to Yvonne.

"Hello, Aunt Beck," Mommy said. "Let's go in and leave the mosquitoes outside."

"You're right, Frances. Come in. I'll heat up supper."

♪ Standing Tall ♪

Melody and Val both loved visiting Aunt Beck, and her living room was one reason why. Every table and shelf was covered with knickknacks. There were china figurines, tiny dolls, picture frames, and small glass candy dishes filled with an assortment of sweets.

What Melody liked best was that Aunt Beck was not the type of adult who didn't allow kids to look at her special things. Aunt Beck happily let Melody and Val pick up anything they liked, and she had a story to tell about each object.

"Oh, girls!" Aunt Beck said. "My grandson Jimmy just sent me a doll all the way from Japan. Wait until you see it!"

Poppa rolled his eyes as he attempted to carry the suitcases through the room without knocking anything over.

"Look at this candy dish shaped like a house!" Val said.

Melody smiled at the fact that houses were still on Val's mind.

"Look at all this stuff," Melody said, pointing at a table in the corner. "Everything has an American flag on it." She was impressed by the ceramic bald eagle carrying a flag in its beak.

"Well, the Fourth of July is only five days away,"
Val said. "We'll see our other cousins, and go to the
fireworks."

"And eat peach ice cream," Melody said. She
opened the top of a flag-shaped tin box.

"Candy?" Val asked.

"Chocolate kisses," Melody answered.

"Mmmm . . . it's good to be back in Birmingham,"
Val mumbled through a mouthful of chocolate.

Melody liked the fact that members of the same
family celebrated holidays differently. Back in Detroit,
Daddy would be up early on the Fourth of July to start
the barbecue. Here at Aunt Beck's, her son Clifford
brought over barbecue in the afternoon. In the morning, Aunt Beck peeled peaches and made the custard
for her homemade ice cream.

Melody woke up early to help. But when she got
to the kitchen, ready to work, Aunt Beck insisted she
have breakfast. "You go over there and get yourself a
cinnamon bun."

♪ Standing Tall ♪

Melody did, and then sat at the kitchen table. Aunt Beck was humming a tune that Melody thought she recognized.

"I know that song from school. It's 'America the Beautiful,' isn't it?" Melody started to sing, and so did Aunt Beck.

> *And crown thy good with brotherhood*
> *From sea to shining sea.*

"I think that's the most important part of the song, isn't it?" Aunt Beck said to Melody. "That brotherhood part. That's what we've all got to figure out."

Melody nodded, her mouth full of warm cinnamon bun. She and Aunt Beck talked about Yvonne and the Mississippi Summer Project. When Mommy came in looking for coffee, Melody was telling Aunt Beck about the Challenge to Change.

"Now that President Johnson has signed the Civil Rights Act, I expect we'll see even more changes," Aunt Beck said to Melody. "Good morning, Frances."

"Good morning," Mommy yawned. "Yes, it's wonderful to have a law saying that we're all equal, and have equal rights. That's what we've been marching for and protesting about all this time."

"That's right," Poppa said, coming into the kitchen.

"Now we just have to get everybody to obey the law," Aunt Beck said.

Melody began to understand what her great-aunt meant—America the Beautiful, brotherhood, civil rights. They did all go together.

After Val woke up and had breakfast, she and Melody got to help Aunt Beck make custard. Melody had never broken so many eggs before. Mommy used the extra peaches to make a cobbler. In the afternoon, Aunt Beck's son Clifford, his wife, Katie, and their children and grandchildren arrived. The house was full.

"This can't be little Melody!" Clifford said in a booming voice that sounded very much like Poppa's. "And Val? How come you grew so fast up there in Detroit?"

Melody didn't get many chances to spend time with little kids, and neither did Val—so they had great fun playing tag and peek-a-boo with their much younger cousins. At dusk, Clifford announced that it was time to go find spots to see the fireworks. Aunt Beck stayed home, but everyone else piled into cars.

Melody stood next to Val, speechless over the beauty of the fireworks in the sky over a giant statue called Vulcan. She and Val argued all the way back over which city's celebration was better—Birmingham's or Detroit's.

"Hey, you live in Detroit now," Melody reminded Val. "So you have to be loyal!"

Clifford, a lawyer, looked at the girls in his rear-view mirror. "I say Val can claim dual citizenship."

"What's that?" Melody asked.

"It means she can be a citizen of two places at the same time," Clifford told her. Melody folded her arms and pretended to be upset, while Val laughed.

When Clifford pulled into the driveway, Melody's mother said, "Now why does Aunt Beck have every light on in the house?"

Before anyone could say anything else, Aunt Beck swung the front door open. Her braid hung against her back. She looked worried.

"Frances, Will has been calling and calling!"

"He has?" Melody's mother hurried out of the car

and up the porch steps. "What's wrong?"

"It's Yvonne," Aunt Beck said. "She's been arrested in Mississippi."

Civil Rights

♫ CHAPTER 15 ♫

elody rushed into the house after Mommy. Val, Poppa, and Clifford followed. "You girls stay here," Poppa ordered before hurrying into the kitchen.

Melody and Val sat down in the living room. The TV was on, and somewhere a radio news program was blaring. All the sounds made everything more confusing.

Melody strained to hear what was happening in the kitchen. Her mother must have called home, because Melody heard Mommy say, "Will! Aunt Beck just told me. Have you heard from her? Not since when?"

Melody felt her lip tremble. She couldn't sit still and hurried into the kitchen. Val followed.

Mommy was on the phone, listening to Daddy. Melody crossed the room and tugged on her shirt.

"What's he saying?" she insisted. But Mommy just motioned for her to be quiet.

"Come on, baby," Aunt Beck said, trying to steer Melody and Val out. But Mommy hung up, and Melody turned to face her.

"What happened?" Clifford asked.

"Yvonne called home yesterday to say she'd been arrested for disturbing the peace. Will hasn't heard from her since, and he can't get any answers from the police station in someplace called Meridian."

"What do you want to do?" Poppa asked.

"Go find her!" Melody's mother said. Melody heard determination in her mother's voice, but also fear.

"I want to come with you," Melody said. Her heart was pounding, and her throat felt tight. All she could think of were the civil rights workers who had disappeared. Yvonne was a civil rights worker.

"Let me help," Clifford said. "I'll drive. You don't need to be in Mississippi with a Michigan license plate on your car, Uncle Frank. Some people over there look for any reason to cause trouble for black people."

"All right, all right," Mommy said, grabbing her purse. "We need to go." She turned to Melody and squeezed her hand. "You'll have to stay here with Aunt Beck."

Then they were gone.

"Are you okay?" Val asked gently.

Melody only nodded. Her throat hurt, and she didn't feel like talking. Aunt Beck tried to convince her to sleep, but Melody couldn't. She was too worried. When both Aunt Beck and Val finally went to bed, Melody stayed up. She sat on the edge of the sofa in the living room, staring at the Fourth of July decorations on the coffee table.

She had so many thoughts crammed into her brain at once that she had a headache. *Is Yvonne okay? Is she missing, like those three civil rights workers who disappeared a few weeks ago?* Melody thought of Aunt Beck sounding so pleased that the Civil Rights Act was now a law. But what good was a law if it couldn't keep people safe?

Melody leaned back against the sofa. She tried to focus on the pecan trees at Poppa's old farm, standing strong and tall during a bad storm.

Melody dreamed that her sisters were calling to her across a field of tall grass. "Melody? Melody!"

She opened her eyes to sunlight streaming through Aunt Beck's living room windows. Melody had fallen asleep on the sofa, and now Yvonne was sitting next to her, calling her name.

"Vonnie!" Melody blinked to make sure her sister was real. Yvonne looked tired. Her Afro was tied back with a scarf, and her left wrist was in a cast.

Melody carefully threw her arms around Yvonne. "Are you okay?" she asked, squeezing her sister tightly.

"I'm all right," Yvonne said, squeezing back. "I got banged up a little, that's all. I'll tell you everything, I promise. But right now, I need to sleep."

Yvonne slept well into the afternoon. After church, Clifford's college-age daughter Anne took Melody and Val to visit Val's old neighborhood. Even though Melody was anxious to talk to Yvonne, it was fun to meet some of Val's old friends and see her cousin so happy.

On their way back to Aunt Beck's, Val turned to

Melody. "I think I understand why Poppa misses his farm," she said quietly. "He misses all the good times he had there with his family and his friends. That's what I miss too."

"Mm-hmm," Melody answered. "Now you have a new home and new friends in Detroit, but you won't ever forget the good times and friends you had here in Birmingham, will you?"

"I won't. Not ever."

At Aunt Beck's, Yvonne was awake and dinner was ready. "You just sit right down here, baby," Aunt Beck said to Yvonne, pulling out a chair at the kitchen table. Clifford and Anne joined Melody and Val while Poppa said grace.

"Thanks, Mom," Yvonne said as Mommy placed a plate of food in front of her. "Thank you all."

Melody noticed that her sister was quieter than usual. She picked up her fork with her right hand, and because she was left-handed, she had trouble using it.

"Can I help?" Melody asked quietly.

Yvonne nodded. "Gee, thanks, Dee-Dee."

Anne said what Melody was thinking. "All right. I want to hear it from you. What happened?"

"Well," Yvonne began, watching Melody cut her meat into pieces. "It's not all that complicated. We had our training and orientation in Oxford, Ohio. That's where I learned to work with elementary school kids, helping improve their reading skills. We also got instructions to be calm when we got arrested."

Melody noticed that Yvonne said "when," not "if."

Yvonne continued. "When we got to Mississippi— to Meridian—we went out to invite parents to send their kids to our Freedom School. There were four of us in the car, two white college students and me, going along this tiny unpaved road where the black people in this community lived. The other person with us was a black high school boy who lived in the area."

"That was good," Aunt Beck said. "You were with somebody the people knew."

"Yes, exactly," Yvonne said. "So we were on the front porch of a house, and this family, the teenagers and parents, were really interested in talking to us. They were asking all kinds of questions. That's when the sheriff's car pulled up along the road. No siren, no flashing lights. I don't even know why he was there."

"Was that scary?" Melody asked.

Yvonne took a deep breath. "Yes. But all of us knew what would happen. That part was in our training, too. The sheriff came up and told us that we were disturbing the peace. The man who owned the house was brave enough to tell the sheriff that he *wanted* to talk to us. But the sheriff repeated that we were disturbing the peace and said we were under arrest."

Anne shook her head. "That's just nuts. That's worse than getting turned away at a hotel or restaurant. Those people have a right to talk to whomever they want. And so do you."

"Yes, but the law enforcement in Mississippi is not interested in giving any black people any kind of civil rights," Clifford said.

Yvonne nodded. "The sheriff dragged us off the porch. As he was pulling me, I tripped on the steps. He kept pulling me anyway, and I fell and broke my wrist. He still took us to jail."

"That's horrible!" Val said.

Yvonne turned to Mommy. "I did get my one phone call. That's when I . . . that's when I called home and Lila answered. I told her to tell you and Dad that I was okay. I know that those three freedom workers are still

missing, and I knew that everyone would be worried about me." Yvonne stopped because her voice got
shaky. Melody put her hand on her sister's.

Yvonne smiled at Melody, and then she took a deep
breath. She looked defiant. "I knew my rights, but
I didn't know if I would get out of jail. I didn't know if
I would ever come home. But now I know that I am not
going to stop fighting for freedom."

"I want you to keep fighting," Mommy said. "But
I want you to take care of yourself, too. You need to
take a break and get yourself together."

Yvonne shook her head. "No, Mom. I want to go
back."

Mommy put her fork down. "Yvonne, I don't know
if—"

Melody interrupted. "Mommy, didn't you say that
Yvonne was old enough to make her own choices?"

Everyone was quiet, and Mommy gave Melody a
long look. Mommy sighed. "I did say that."

"I'll be as careful as I can," Yvonne said, "but we all
know the fight isn't over. President Johnson just signed
the Civil Rights Act, but this fight is not on paper."

Aunt Beck cleared her throat. "Yvonne, why don't

you stay here for a few days to rest up? Then Clifford can take you back to Mississippi."

"Thanks, Aunt Beck. I'll stay if Mommy agrees to let me go back to Mississippi."

"Frances," Clifford said to Mommy, "if it makes you feel any better, I have friends in Meridian who can keep an eye on her."

Mommy nodded. "It does. But let me talk to Will about it tonight. For now, let's enjoy being with one another. All right?"

"That sounds fine," Aunt Beck said. "Now, I've got peach cobbler just waiting to get eaten up!"

Yvonne leaned toward Melody. "Thanks," she whispered.

"You're welcome," Melody whispered back.

"Girls," Mommy said. "Those were stage whispers."

For the next few days, Melody didn't leave Yvonne's side. She helped Yvonne do anything she couldn't do because of her cast. Yvonne rested a lot, but she and Melody talked a lot, too. Melody told her all about the trip to the Motown studio and how amazing it had been to see Dwayne as a real musician. She described Poppa's farm and how she had pictured Mommy as a girl growing up there. Yvonne asked Melody lots of questions about her park project, and she was impressed that Melody had thought to write a letter to Martha Jean the Queen. "That's makin' it work, Dee-Dee," she'd said.

Daddy had agreed that Yvonne could go back to Meridian on the condition that she call home every few days. So early on Thursday morning, everyone left Birmingham at the same time. Melody walked Yvonne to Clifford's car.

"I know this has been scary for you," Yvonne said, gesturing to the cast on her wrist, "but I'm glad we got a chance to see each other."

"Me, too," Melody said. "I'm glad you're okay."

"I am okay. And I'm not doing this alone. Neither are you, Dee-Dee," Yvonne said gently. "Remember. You came up with a great plan for the park, and you found great kids to work with. Trust them."

"Okay," Melody promised as Yvonne got in the car.

"And don't forget to send me pictures of that playground!" Yvonne yelled as Clifford pulled away.

Keep Going

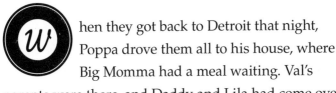

hen they got back to Detroit that night, Poppa drove them all to his house, where Big Momma had a meal waiting. Val's parents were there, and Daddy and Lila had come over for supper, too. Even Dwayne joined them. Everyone wanted to hear about the trip.

"So, Frances," Charles said, sitting down at the dining room table, "what happened with Yvonne?"

"I kind of want to know the answer to that question, too," Dwayne said, looking at his mother. "Is she safe down there?"

"I admit, I've been worried about Yvonne ever since I heard the news reports about those three young men who went missing," Big Momma said, folding her hands together.

Tish shook her head. "I just don't think we could

ever allow Valerie to do something like what Yvonne is doing."

"Wait a minute," Daddy said. "We all care about our children, and we care about the world they grow up in, don't we?"

Charles nodded. "That's true, Will."

Tish nodded, too. She started to say something else, but Mommy put both her hands in the air.

"Listen, everyone. We have a freedom fighter. Her name is Yvonne Marie Ellison. She has decided to go where we will not go—" Mommy looked at Melody. "Or cannot yet go, to lift her voice and use her gifts to try to make the world better for all of us. Every day there are black people and white people putting themselves in harm's way to change the world." Mommy's voice was shaking. "And I am so very, very proud of my Yvonne!"

Daddy got up, walked around the table, and put his arm around Mommy's shoulders. "Ditto," was all he said.

"Wow. Mom and Dad have got Yvonne's back." Dwayne whispered to Lila. Lila nodded.

Melody was so very, very proud of all of them.

♪ Keep Going ♪

Melody was up early the next morning, and she dressed quickly so that she could go check on the playground. She was anxious to see how everything looked after her time away.

Bo was excited that Melody was home, and he ran around her in circles in the kitchen. She clipped his leash onto his collar and said, "Okay. You can come with me."

Outside, Bo barked and pulled at the leash. He knew exactly where he was going. As they rounded the corner by the park, Melody's heart beat fast. She saw the tall stems of the hollyhocks and daylilies standing at attention. The morning sun had already opened many of the lilies' orange flowers, and the hollyhocks looked like bright red ruffles.

As she swung the park gate open, Melody did a double take. It didn't creak! Someone had oiled the hinges.

To her surprise, Diane and Sharon were already at work in the vegetable patch.

"Hi!" Melody called out.

"Melody!" Sharon stood up to run over, but then she took a look at her dirty shorts and shirt, and simply laughed.

"Hey, Melody." Diane pushed back the sun hat she was wearing. Behind her was a tall bamboo tepee with green-bean vines carefully wound around each slender stick.

"Nice beans," Melody said.

Diane grinned. "I've kind of started to like gardening," she said. "Look! The beans have *flowers* on them!" She pointed to the tiny white blossoms.

"Yes, they do," Melody said. "We—I mean, you— will have green beans soon. That's great!"

"Take a look around and check things out," Sharon said. "We've been working really hard."

Melody was pleased to see that the flower beds had been weeded and watered. The red geraniums were perky, and the tiny impatiens looked like mounds of orange, pink, and white popcorn. She glanced at the morning glory vines climbing up the swing supports. It was still disappointing not to have swings, but the trumpet-shaped flowers would be cheerful when they bloomed.

♪ Keep Going ♪

"It's looking good, huh?"

Melody turned to see Julius and his friend Larry. Julius was wearing gardening gloves. "Welcome back," he said. "Larry and I just stopped by to do a little weeding."

Melody tilted her head to see that Larry was carrying a ball.

"Well, we want to break in the handball courts before the opening," Julius said with a shrug.

Melody laughed. "It looks great. I can't wait for the picnic, so everyone can see what we've done."

"Three weeks and counting!" Julius said, heading off with Larry.

Melody wrote down a few things in her notebook. There were some bare spots in the flower border in back, and she wanted to get some plants to fill them in. And the hopscotch grids hadn't been painted on the paths yet. Other than that, all they had to do was keep weeding, pinch back the dead blooms so the plants continued to flower, and make sure everything was watered.

"Not bad, Bo," she said as they turned to leave. "Not bad at all!"

Val's garden hadn't fared so well. When Val called in a panic, Mommy agreed to drive Melody to Val's house. Val met Melody on the front porch.

"You have to help," she said, taking Melody's hand and dragging her through the house. "It's a disaster!"

"It can't be that bad," Melody said. But when Val pulled her out the back door, all Melody could say was, "Oh."

"See?" Val almost squealed.

The pink impatiens that the girls had planted in neat borders around the trees were wilting. The pots of purple petunias they'd set along the back steps looked shriveled. The tomatoes in the vegetable bed on the sunny side of the yard had several yellowing leaves.

"I don't understand what happened," Val said.

"Not enough water," Melody replied. "Where's your hose?"

"Over here," Val said, leading Melody to the side of the house, where a green garden hose was neatly coiled. "But it's so heavy. Besides, I thought it would rain."

Melody made a face. "You mean, you were waiting for rain? You didn't even water things before we left?"

Val stood still. "That wasn't right?"

Melody shook her head.

"But I never see you watering with a hose," Val said.

Melody unwound the hose. "That's because I do it early in the morning, before it gets too hot, or late in the afternoon, after the sun goes down."

"I'm a bad gardener," Val said.

"Nope." Melody handed her the hose. "Just a new one. You'll learn. Let's give them a good drink now."

"So my tomatoes still have a chance?"

"Of course they do," Melody said with a smile, turning on the faucet.

In church the Sunday before the picnic, Pastor Daniels made an announcement. "Some of our fine young people have answered the New Year's challenge with good works."

He made the five of them stand up in front of the congregation. "I asked them to use their gifts to make justice, equality, and dignity grow," Pastor

Daniels went on. "They did so by making an entire *garden* grow! Well done, Junior Block Club." Everyone applauded, and Melody and her friends beamed.

On Monday evening, Melody went over plans with Mr. Sterling, who was on the picnic planning committee. Every year, the club got permission from the city to close off a block to traffic. Neighbors set up tables and grills and brought food to share. Sometimes there was music, and this year the Junior Block Club was in charge of that. Sharon had drawn several posters promoting The Three Ravens, and Poppa and Mr. Sterling put them in their shops.

Tuesday started out bright and sunny as Melody headed over to the park with Bo and a wagon full of marigolds that Poppa had given her to fill in the bare spots. Sharon was there to paint the hopscotch grids, and Diane was checking the vegetables. They all sang and hummed while they worked.

By the time Melody headed home, it had gotten cloudy. "Looks like rain, Bo," she said, scooping him up into the wagon and running. "Let's move fast." Bo barked as the wagon bumped along the sidewalk. They made it home just as the rain began to pelt down.

♪ Keep Going ♪

Mommy was reading when Melody came in. "How's the garden?" she asked, sipping her coffee.

"Perfect," Melody said, wiping her wet sneakers on the doormat. "And the rain is just what all the plants need to look great this weekend."

Melody didn't know that the rain would turn into a storm.

Lila stomped in soaking wet, and later their father came home from work the same way. It was cozy inside. Daddy went to bed early, as usual, but Mommy stayed up with Melody and Lila and played board games. They listened to Dwayne's record over and over and tried to ignore the thunder.

But the fun didn't keep Melody from worrying about the weather. It rained through the night and all the next day. The wind blew and the rain pounded, and the windows of the house rattled. On the second night there was lightning.

By Thursday morning the storm had passed. When Melody turned on her radio, the weatherman was saying that there might have been a tornado.

"A tornado? In Detroit?" Lila mumbled sleepily. "What is he talking about?"

Melody hopped out of bed and went to the window. "Well, I see a huge branch down in the yard behind ours, and the lawn chairs are all over the place. I hope the playground is okay," she said, getting dressed quickly.

Melody hurried downstairs to find her mother and grandfather sitting at the kitchen table.

"Where are you off to?" Mommy asked.

"I want to make sure everything at the garden and playground is all right," Melody said. "May I?"

"Why don't I go with you," Poppa said, putting on his cap. "I noticed quite a few big branches down on my way over here."

"Thanks, Poppa."

A few minutes later, Melody was tiptoeing around puddles on the sidewalk and holding her breath as she went in through the silent gate.

"Oh, no!" she cried.

An enormous branch from one of the trees along the edge of the playground had split and fallen. It blocked two of the three handball courts. "I'll find someone to help move that," Poppa said.

But that was just one part of the playground. The

rest was littered with twigs and leaves. Most of the geraniums had lost their clusters of red petals, and the bare stems were bent low. The morning glory vines had blown completely off the swing supports and were trailing on the ground. The green-bean tepees in the vegetable garden had toppled over. The hopscotch grids had disappeared in the storm.

"Poppa, it's ruined!" Melody moaned. "We can't possibly fix all this before the picnic! What will we do?"

Poppa patted Melody's shoulder. "Nature fixes itself, Little One. You clean up as best you can, and then you wait. Wait for sun, wait for the strong roots of these plants to keep growing down under the earth. They're anchored, remember? And as long as those roots remain strong, they will continue to grow."

Melody was discouraged. "We were all done, Poppa," she sighed.

"A garden is never finished," Poppa said gently. "Gardens—and good works—keep going, but they both need tending. Keep tending the garden. Keep contributing to your community. Keep going."

Melody went home to think. Yvonne had told her to trust the people she was working with. So she called Diane and told her about the park. "I need help," Melody said.

"We need hands!" Diane said. "Let me call around. I'll call you back." She clicked off.

Melody called Val, Sharon, and Julius, and they all said the same thing: "I'll be right over."

A short time later, Melody and the other four original members of the Junior Block Club stood and looked at the mess.

"Man!" Julius whistled. "It sure looks like a tornado hit! Look at that branch on the handball court!" He started toward it.

"Wait," Melody said. "You mean it's on the new brick wall?"

Julius scrambled through the leaves. "Yeah! Knocked out some of the bricks, too."

Melody shook her head. "My grandfather is going to move the branch, but there's no way we can get the bricks fixed by Saturday."

"People can still play on the courts, if we clear them out," Julius said.

♪ Keep Going ♪

Melody sighed. "Let's clean up the paths first."

"How can I help?" a voice behind them asked.

"Miss Esther!" Melody rushed to hug her. "Thank you for coming!"

"I'm here to work," Miss Esther said. "Where do you want me to start?"

Melody was about to answer when she saw a group of people appear at the gate. There were at least twenty kids from school and around the neighborhood. Some of them had rakes and brooms, and others carried garbage bags.

"What's going on?" Val asked.

"More hands," Diane said. "I asked a few people to help."

"Wow," Sharon whispered.

Melody smiled. "Okay," she said. "Let's keep going."

A Playground and a Party

*m*elody could hardly believe it, but on Saturday, the playground was ready for a party. So many people had shown up to help on Thursday that all the branches and debris had been cleared from the paths. Most of the flowers had bounced back after a full Friday of sun. The morning glory vines hadn't survived the storm, so Melody and Miss Esther had trimmed them back. When Sharon had painted the fresh set of hopscotch grids on the path, she had surprised Melody by painting images of morning glories along the edges.

As she got dressed that morning, Melody looked at the wish list that she and Miss Esther had made as well as the plan for the playground that Sharon had drawn. Both pieces of paper were taped to the wall above Melody's bed. The real playground didn't look exactly like the drawing, and there were things on the wish list that were still just wishes. But since Poppa had said that a garden is never finished, Melody decided that a playground never is, either.

The Junior Block Club was meeting at the park at one o'clock to blow up the balloons that Poppa supplied for the party every year. At five minutes to one, Melody gathered her bags and called upstairs. "I'm going."

"We'll be there soon," Mommy called back down. "I've just got to pack up the food."

It was a perfect day to be outside. As soon as Melody got to the end of her block, she could see where the street had been blocked off. Neighbors were setting up card tables and lawn chairs in the road and putting coolers in the shade.

When she got to the park, Julius was standing at the gate, wearing a new striped T-shirt.

"Hey," he said, taking one of the bags from Melody.

"Hey, Julius." Melody grinned. "Thanks."

A minute later, Sharon came running from one direction while Diane arrived from the other. Val showed up with her mom. "We brought string for the balloons," Val called.

The group headed into the park, and Melody was happy to see that the playground was already busy. Some girls were playing jacks near the morning glory hopscotch paths, and a father was helping his little boy on the jungle gym. Kids were zipping down the slide and then running back to the ladder to take another turn.

Dwayne and his bandmates were setting up a mini stage next to the handball courts. There were big speakers and a couple of microphones. Artie was fiddling with wires and a large tape recorder, and Phil was standing to one side talking to Lila. Melody walked over to her sister.

"I didn't know you'd be here already," Melody said.

"Well, um," Lila stammered, "I thought you might need some help with the balloons."

Melody grinned. "Sure. C'mon over," she teased before turning to Dwayne.

"What do you think of the setup?" Dwayne asked. "We recorded the instrumentals last night, but we'll be singing live today."

"This is great," she said. "I'm really glad you're here."

"You didn't think I'd miss this, did you?" Dwayne
tugged at Melody's braid. She grinned and hurried
back to her friends. Sharon and Julius were blowing up
the balloons. Tish was cutting lengths of string from
a spool, and Val and Diane were tying them to the
balloons.

Melody took a big bunch of balloons to the front
of the park and was tying them to the gate when
Miss Esther made her way across the street. "Hello
there, Melody," she called. "I see everything is in fine
bloom, thanks to you!"

"Thanks to all of us," Melody said.

The park and the street in front of it began to fill,
and soon it seemed as though the whole neighborhood
was outside. Poppa and Big Momma and all the parents
of the Junior Block Club members arrived at the playground at the same time.

"I think they planned this," Sharon said.

"We did," her mother answered. "We want to take a
picture of you five. We're so proud of all you've done."

At that moment, Dwayne spoke into a microphone.
"Hello, neighbors," he said. "How about a hand for the
Junior Block Club that worked so hard to clean up our

park!" When the kids were all up onstage, Dwayne introduced them each by name. The crowd hooted and cheered, and all the moms took out cameras.

"Over here," Mommy said.

"Look this way," Diane's mother called.

"I thought you said *a* picture," Sharon sighed.

"Hey, who is that?" Julius asked, pointing.

Melody saw a glamorous-looking lady step through the park gate, nodding and waving to the crowd.

"Who *is* that?" Melody asked.

"I know!" Diane said. "It's Martha Jean the Queen, from WCHB radio."

Melody couldn't believe it. Lots of people had contacted the Parks Department about their play-ground because they'd heard about it on Martha Jean's radio show. And all the phone calls and letters were what had prompted the Parks Department to take off the padlock. But Melody had never expected Miss Martha Jean to come to the park's grand opening. How did she even know about it?

"Look!" Melody whispered. Martha Jean was heading straight for the stage.

"Ladies and gentlemen," Dwayne said into the

microphone. "It looks like we have a special guest. Miss Martha Jean Steinberg, the Queen of Detroit radio!"

Everyone applauded. Miss Martha Jean smiled for Tish's flashing camera before she strode across the stage in her high heels to stand next to Dwayne.

"Melody Ellison?" Miss Martha Jean called out.

Melody's eyes grew wide. Dwayne motioned her over to the microphone. "Yes, ma'am?" Melody said, standing between her brother and Miss Martha Jean.

"So you're the young lady who wrote me about the playground project! Well, Melody, I came here today in person to congratulate you on your persistence, your dedication to your community, and . . ." she glanced around, "your hard work!" The crowd clapped again.

"Th-Thank you," Melody said.

"And I have some words from our mayor, the Honorable Jerome Cavanagh."

"The mayor?"

Martha Jean nodded. "I have a proclamation to read." She held up what looked like a picture frame with a letter under the glass. "Miss Ellison," the Queen's radio voice rang out. "On behalf of the City of Detroit, we thank you and the Junior Block Club for your service to the community, and hereby officially re-open the Junior Block Club Children's Park and Playground!"

Melody was stunned. The park had been named for the Junior Block Club! And the mayor knew her name! Melody heard the audience clapping as the other Junior Block Club members and their parents hooted and stomped.

"Thank you, Miss Queen," Melody said. "I mean, Miss The Queen . . . I mean . . ." She blinked and focused on the faces of her family.

Martha Jean patted her shoulder and laughed. "I think we should thank Melody for changing this park and playground into a beautiful place for all of us, and for being responsible enough to see it through!"

Now everyone began to cheer. Melody felt overwhelmed, but there was something important that she needed to say. She leaned into the microphone.

"Thank you," Melody said. She waited for the crowd to quiet. "But I didn't do this all myself. The playground changes only got done because lots of people made suggestions and gave advice." Melody looked at Poppa and Miss Esther, who were standing with Melody's parents. "And lots of people did the work." Melody waved the rest of the Junior Block Club over to stand by her. "There were also lots of neighborhood kids who helped, so thank you to them, too."

Everyone cheered again, and Tish took more pictures.

"Well, there's one more thing, Miss Ellison," Martha Jean said. "Since we got so many calls and pledges of support at the station, I would like to present to the Junior Block Club this check for seventy-five dollars, to cover some of the cost of getting new swings for your playground. Congratulations, and please continue your good work, all of you!"

Melody was so full of feelings that she couldn't respond with words, so she hugged Miss Martha Jean to thank her. Then she took the check and filed off the stage with the rest of her friends.

Martha Jean stayed at the microphone and introduced Dwayne's group. "And now, our neighborhood Motown stars, The Three Ravens, will perform a song that's destined to be a hit."

The Queen suddenly stopped talking, and Melody turned back toward the stage to see why.

Dwayne had taken the microphone. "I'd like to ask my sister to come back up here," he said, motioning to Melody.

Melody's eyes met Dwayne's. "Me?" she mouthed.

Dwayne nodded. Then the music began and the audience went wild.

Melody stood still for a moment, smiling. Then she walked back to the stage along the hopscotch path, past some of the daylilies, past her parents' and grandparents' proud faces.

She thought about how hard Dwayne had worked to make his record, how hard Lila always studied, and about the hard work Yvonne and so many others were doing to help justice and equality grow.

As she took a spot onstage beside her brother, Melody realized that her little idea of fixing up the playground had grown into something bigger and more beautiful than she'd ever imagined. She began to bounce happily to the music, raising her voice to sing with Dwayne. Melody knew the lyrics by heart, but today, they meant something different to her.

It's time for me to shine,
Make the jump to the big time.
Hit the road at a run,
Dance and jump and have some fun.
You know what that's gotta mean?
Girl, it's time that I move,
Time for movin' on up.

Melody knew in her heart that she would always remember this song, this place, and this day.

INSIDE Melody's World

When Melody answered Pastor Daniels's call to make things better in her community, she formed a Junior Block Club and helped create a beautiful park. What Melody did in her neighborhood was exactly what civil rights activists were doing across the country: taking action. One example was the Mississippi Summer Project. In the South, African Americans were not allowed to vote, so they had no say in their local government. It was dangerous for black people to try to change things. They could get arrested, fired from their jobs, thrown out of their homes, or even killed. Civil rights organizations wanted to help, so they came together for what became known as Freedom Summer.

The goal of Freedom Summer was to support black people as they exercised their rights and to help them overcome the fear of violence. Hundreds of college students from the North—both black and white—went to Mississippi. They helped adults register to vote, and they set up schools and community centers for kids. Melody's sister Yvonne volunteered as one of the teachers. She went door to door inviting children of all ages to Freedom School. Black residents welcomed the college students. One woman was happy to discover that the white students "were just like anyone else."

Classes took place on front porches, under trees, and in church basements. Like Yvonne, most of the teachers had never taught before. But they were eager to help the kids learn how to read, write, and do math. They led classes in black history, the civil rights movement, and leadership skills. At night, there were classes for adults.

Melody was proud of her sister for joining Freedom Summer. But she was worried about her, too. Volunteers were harassed, arrested, and even attacked. Three of the workers, James Chaney, Michael Schwerner, and Andrew Goodman, disappeared on June 21. Their bodies were found on August 4. Although several members of the Ku Klux Klan, a violent hate group, were responsible for killing the three activists, only one man was found guilty of murder. It took over 40 years to convict him.

As Freedom Summer began, an important bill was signed into law. On July 2, 1964, the Civil Rights Act made segregation in public places illegal in every part of the country. Restaurants, movie theaters, parks, hotels, and stores could no longer refuse to serve black people or make them sit in separate sections or use separate entrances. Although the law was passed, change did not happen overnight. It took months, and even years, before some public places provided black people with equal service.

The civil rights movement is not over. Americans have made great progress by ending legal segregation, but many people still face discrimination because of the color of their skin. People of all races and ages continue to take action to make justice, equality, and dignity grow.

Read more of MELODY'S stories,

available from booksellers and at *americangirl.com*

♪ *Classics* ♪

Melody's classic series, now in two volumes:

Volume 1:
No Ordinary Sound

Melody can't wait to sing her first solo at church. She spends the summer practicing the perfect song—and helping her brother become a Motown singer. When an unimaginable tragedy leaves her silent, Melody has to find her voice.

Volume 2:
Never Stop Singing

Now that her brother is singing for Motown, Melody gets to visit a real recording studio. She also starts a children's Block Club. Melody is determined to help her neighborhood bloom—and make her community stronger.

♪ *Journey in Time* ♪

Travel back in time—and spend a few days with Melody!

Music in My Heart

Step into Melody's world of the 1960s! Volunteer with a civil rights group, join a demonstration, or use your voice to sing backup for a Motown musician! Choose your own path through this multiple-ending story.

♫ A Sneak Peek at ♫

Music in My Heart

My Journey with Melody

Meet Melody and take a journey back in time in a book that lets *you* decide what happens.

It's funny how one song can change *everything.*

I'm sitting at the piano on Saturday afternoon, playing my recital piece again. The *tick, tick, tick* of the metronome keeps my fingers moving, but my mind wanders. *One more piano recital*, I remind myself. *Then on to guitar!* Our fifth-grade class will learn guitar at school this fall. I can picture it now . . . my best friend, Anika, and me jamming together. Bye-bye, classical music. Hello, pop!

The metronome grows louder. Then I realize that the sound is actually my piano teacher, clapping her hands to get my attention. "Stop, stop, stop . . ." Ms. Stricker scolds. She's frowning. Anika and I don't call her "Ms. Strict" for nothing!

My hands drop to my lap. "Did I make a mistake?" I ask.

"No," she says. "You're playing the notes perfectly. But there's no *passion* in the piece—your heart's not in it."

She sounds like my dad, who is always telling me to "find my passion." He's a politician, so he's really passionate about helping people and making a

difference in our community. *But what's my passion?*
I wonder. I'm not so sure it's piano. Sometimes when
I read music, it flows straight from my eyes to my
fingertips. It must skip my brain, because I can think
about something else while I'm playing. *Maybe it
skips my heart, too,* I think sadly. "Sorry," I say to
Ms. Stricker, trying not to stare at the mole above her
left eyebrow. If I blur my eyes, it looks like a quarter
note without the stem.

Ms. Stricker sighs. She checks the clock on top of
the piano. "I think," she says, "it's time for a different
song."

A different song? The recital is only two weeks
away! As Ms. Stricker rummages around in her
cabinet, I hum the melody of my new favorite song,
"Lemonade Days." I can't hit the high notes like Zoey
Gatz does in her music video, but Anika can. I wish
Ms. Stricker would let me play *that* song!

Instead, she hands me an old, stained piece of
music with dog-eared corners. The title is "Lift Every
Voice and Sing." "Try this one," she says.

As my fingers find the notes, the music takes
shape. It sounds like the gospel songs my grandma

and I used to sing at her church. As I play the slow, soulful song, I feel a pang of sadness. Grammy died a few months ago. I can almost hear her singing the first line: *"Lift every voice and sing, till earth and heaven ring."*

When I reach the second verse, something happens. That single voice in my head swells, joined by other voices. I glance up from the keys, expecting to see a room full of people. There's no one there.

I can't hear the metronome anymore. I don't hear the phone ring either. When Ms. Stricker says she'll be right back—that she has to take a call—I keep playing. It's as if I can't stop.

"Let us march on till victory is won," the imaginary choir sings. And my fingers march on, too, across the keys. My heart speeds up, urging me toward the end of the song.

As I play the final note, I feel a breeze. The sheet music flutters, and the room darkens, as if someone pulled a curtain. I see nothing except the blue numbers on the digital clock, blinking 1:26, 1:26, 1:26. Then it all fades away.

I rub my eyes. The sheet music is still in front of me, but everything else has changed. There's a clock on the piano, but it's round and squat, with two bells on top. And this isn't Ms. Stricker's piano at all! Hers is made of shiny mahogany, almost red. This piano is lighter and covered with a fine layer of dust.

There's a bulletin board hanging above the piano. My eyes are drawn to a familiar face—a black man— staring out from a poster. "Walk to Freedom with Dr. Martin Luther King Jr.," the poster reads. I squint to read the print at the bottom: "Detroit, Michigan. Sunday, June 23, 1963."

"Wow!" says a girl's voice from behind me.

I whirl around. She's standing in the doorway: a girl about my age wearing a sleeveless green-and-blue-checked dress that pops against her golden brown skin. The dress is short and flares out at the hem. It reminds me of the dress my grandma is wearing in a photo of her as a teenager.

"That was *amazing*," the girl says.

What is she talking about? I wonder, turning back to the poster. "The, um, Walk to Freedom, you mean?" I stammer.

She laughs. "No, silly—your piano playing!" she says. "But the Walk to Freedom here in Detroit last summer was pretty amazing, too. My family and I marched in it."

Last summer? The poster says that the Walk to Freedom happened in June of 1963. I do the math. That was more than fifty years ago.

Then I notice the room around me. It's filled with fold-up tables and chairs, like a meeting hall. On the table closest to me, I see an old typewriter. My mom has one in her office, but just for decoration. It's too hard to press down on those raised keys. There's a black telephone on the table, too, with a long, twisted cord. My grandma had one like that in her apartment.

Everything in this room seems old-fashioned, like a scene from a black-and-white movie. A question swirls through my mind. *Is this my craziest daydream ever, or did I just play my way back in time?*

"I'm Melody," says the girl in the doorway, "I *love* the song you just played. So does my grandma. She's here at church. If I go get her, will you play it again?"

Her brown eyes smile at me from beneath her turquoise headband. She's real. This can't be a daydream!

"Please?" she asks.

When I nod, the girl spins on her heel. I hear her footsteps clattering up a set of stairs.

I try to remember the last time anyone seemed so happy to hear me play piano. Definitely not Ms. Strict at lessons this afternoon! But there *is* something special about the song I just finished. My fingers stroke the keys again, softly at first. But after the first verse, I barely need to read the music. I sail through it, hearing the voices rise up around me.

> *Sing a song full of the faith*
> *that the dark past has taught us,*
> *Sing a song full of the hope*
> *that the present has brought us.*

I close my eyes and let the music fill me up. As the last notes fade away, I hear a *tick, tick, tick*. I open my eyes and see the silver bar of Ms. Stricker's metronome. It swings from side to side, as if gesturing toward the clock on the piano—the clock with blue numbers that still read 1:26.

When Ms. Stricker steps into the room, I jump. Then I see the expression on her face. She's actually smiling.

"That was beautiful," she says—for the first time ever. I've heard her say "perfect," but never "beautiful."

Pride swells in my chest, followed by excitement. I did it again! I played this magical song and somehow traveled through time. Then I think of Melody, that mysterious girl I left behind. My fingers itch to play the song again and get back to her in that basement room.

"Your mom will be here in a couple of minutes," Ms. Stricker says. "Take the music home with you, my dear. Polish it up and make it yours."

I place the music carefully in my book bag. This song already feels like mine, more than anything else I've ever played. *Wait for me, Melody,* I think, trying to send a message across time. *I'll be back soon!*

About the Author

DENISE LEWIS PATRICK grew up in the town of Natchitoches, Louisiana. Lots of relatives lived nearby, so there was always someone watching out for her and always someone to play with. Every week, Denise and her brother went to the library, where she would read and dream in the children's room overlooking a wonderful river. She wrote and illustrated her first book when she was ten—she glued yellow cloth to cardboard for the cover and sewed the pages together on her mom's sewing machine. Today, Denise lives in New Jersey, but she loves returning to her hometown and taking her four sons to all the places she enjoyed as a child.

Advisory Board

American Girl extends its deepest appreciation
to the advisory board that authenticated Melody's stories.

Julian Bond

Chairman Emeritus, NAACP Board of Directors, and founding
member of Student Nonviolent Coordinating Committee (SNCC)

Rebecca de Schweinitz

Associate Professor of History, Brigham Young University,
and author of *If We Could Change the World: Young People and
America's Long Struggle for Racial Equality* (Chapel Hill:
University of North Carolina Press, 2009)

Gloria House

Director and Professor Emerita, African and African American
Studies, University of Michigan–Dearborn, and SNCC Field
Secretary, Lowndes County, Alabama, 1963-1965

Juanita Moore

President and CEO of Charles H. Wright Museum of
African American History, Detroit, and founding executive director
of the National Civil Rights Museum, Memphis, Tennessee

Thomas J. Sugrue

Professor of History, New York University, and author of
*Sweet Land of Liberty: The Forgotten Struggle for Civil Rights
in the North* (Random House, 2008)

JoAnn Watson

Native of Detroit, ordained minister, and former
executive director of the Detroit NAACP